CELTIC, the Prequel
vol.1
by D. J. HIGHLANDER

Title | CELTIC, the Prequel - vol.1
Author | D. J. Highlanders

ISBN | 978-88-27830-86-4

Youcanprint Self-Publishing
Via Roma, 73 – 73039 Tricase (LE) – Italy
www.youcanprint.it
info@youcanprint.it
Facebook: facebook.com/youcanprint.it
Twitter: twitter.com/youcanprintit

PREFACE

'Upyerockye'.

Charlie's bagpipe precedes the roll of the three drums, played by his bandmates. A slow rhythm, suddenly building up. Then the bagpipe fades out, leaving room for the drums and the electric guitar in the background. Some time later, joining the rhythm of the cheers, Charlie comes back to the ensemble in a traditional Scottish apparel and full grey beard, to accompany his friends with his bagpipe until the very last moment, the last roll, the last breath, down to a sudden stop.
The audience, a hundred people or so, gave a huge round of applause at the band, shouting and singing. Saor Patrol, a Scottish band from Edinburgh, were so good the were intoxicating. I couldn't but go to the stand and buy their new album.

Milan, first days of December. The craft fair is about to end, and the band has been here since day one, singing three of their hits on the stage of Spirit of the Planet, an association promoting the traditional and ethnic cultures of native peoples of the Earth.
Still lost in their beautiful music, after the concert I took the car and drove back to my native town. On

the way I played the cd I bought at the fair. When the notes of 'Upyerockye' came out the amps of the car sound system, a picture shaped up in my head that would keep me company until I finally got home.

A boy in the woods, fleeing from other people. He runs, slides, falls, gets up and runs again, tailed by those people, those enemies. Until...

This was the spark that brought 'Celtic' to life.
Before I started writing some days passed. I'd never thought about writing a novel, but this scene, its image, the atmosphere, everything of it was so clear in my mind, that writing it all down came almost natural.

Of course I had no idea where to begin, what with such an intricate plot, but places, characters, events kept popping into my head one after the other.
When in the end I decided I couldn't keep it in anymore, I burst into writing. Twenty days later I was writing the words 'the End' to the first book.

What is 'Celtic'? I'll let the readers find that out on their own.
It's an adventure, a great adventure that allows the mind to go over the horizon and cross every bind. Sky's the limit, and breaking that limit the reader can

taste that particular freedom no one can really describe. The Celtic freedom.

It's been seven years since I wrote the first novel. Meanwhile it was proofread by Prof. Andrea Vitali, human scientist, medieval historian, musicologist, world's greatest expert in medieval iconography and symbolism and creator of the Cultural Association 'Le Tarot'. After his proofread, encouraged by his great interest in my work, I tried to pitch it to a selection of Italian publishing houses with absolutely no success. In late 2017 I finally managed to find a way to self-publish it, but in all this time something had changed.

During these years of wait, it became clearer and clearer to me that what 'Celtic' lacked, and surely needs is an introduction of some sort. A preamble, introducing the answers to some issues the readers will come to face in the various volumes of the novel, that would otherwise be left unanswered for lack of space. To this purpose, before I release the first volume of 'Celtic', I have decided to collect some short side stories in the form of a prequel, which I hope will make the readers' immersion into the atmosphere and universe of 'Celtic' much more gradual and comfortable.

Pilot
The LIBRARY

"When it all begun, you ask? It's hard to say. I think the closest thing to the truth is to assume we always existed, ever since mankind walked the Earth for the very first time. You see, these lands always exuded our culture, our way of life, the force – or spirit, if you prefer – of our tradition. We were always here. No matter how many times other peoples tried to extirpate us, annihilate us or rob us of our lands. Even though today there isn't in our blood the biological root of the primeval inhabitants of these lands, sooner or later our strength, our essence and spirit would permeate all of those who came here, and they would become one with us. We are this ground we live on, the strength of this region, the unity of a universe destined to survive the millennia, and though we endured destruction again and again, every time we have grown back greater and stronger. Nowadays, something in our world is changing, and we cannot remain oblivious to it nor observe the changes in silence.

We cannot hide in fear of a new Era of destruction. We want to come out of the shadows and live in the light again, and finally we have enough strength to get what we want for ourselves."

The old man finished his monologue and turned his gaze towards his listener, a correspondent for the Irish Times, who had been walking behind him scribbling on his notepad trough the entire Village and was now following him into a traditional wooden house, end of the tour and home to the library.

"Of course I understand your fervor perfectly, when I asked you to begin from the start however, I didn't mean that far back… it would take, like, literally an Era, and I only have a couple of columns for this piece, you know."

The old man looked at the journalist, a young lad rather uninterestingly recording the interview on his smartphone, then moved his gaze to the floor. The wooden floorboards of a warm brown rosewood captured him as always with their alternate violet brown and purplish grains.

"All right, then. What would you like to know?"

"Eh, so. Well… I don't know. Something – something like how you got where you got. The Village, the places where your people originally came from, the reasons why they came here, to… this."

"I sincerely doubt two columns will be enough for you to cover all that. What you ask is huge, each of those questions deserves a properly developed answer. Your two columns won't suffice." answered the old man, beginning to lose his patience.

"You choose, then. Just let me do my job, alright?"

The white haired old man brought his right hand to his chin, stroking the long snow-white beard with thin, delicate fingers, lost in his thoughts. Suddenly he lit up.
"I might have just what you need. Why don't you write about our library?"

"Your library. I'm sorry, but what would I write about it, exactly? 'There were four bookcases in a room'…" teased the journalist. He really couldn't believe the man.

"Four bookcases in a room? Oh, come on. You wouldn't think this room we're in is the whole library, wouldn't you?" said the old man winking at the visitor. "This is but the entrance, the lobby, the place where books await to be registered and assigned to their rightful place in the library's collection. Come with me, I'll show you the library!"

The journalist followed the old man, still unconvinced of how a library, although kept by those weirdos on whom everybody seemed to have something to comment all the time, could become of any interest to the editor in chief of the most read newspaper in Dublin.

"Here we are!" exclaimed the old man showing the journalist to a chair at the long, dark red, solid wooden table dominating the centre of the room they had just entered.

Tens of thousands of books were crammed top to bottom along the four meters high walls, in a maniacally catalogued and sorted out chaos. The reporter sat heavily on the exquisitely chiseled wooden chair, decorated with the incision of a hundreds years old oak. He left the smartphone on the table and snapped at the old man:
"You have no shortages of books here, for sure!"

"You think? Actually, this is but the tip of the iceberg. We are in the smallest of twelve book storage chambers, all located in this very building, two floors above us and four floors below. And then we have an auditorium, twelve reading rooms…"

"Where do all these books come from? I mean, the money to build such a collection… How could you possibly get it?" asked the journalist, mesmerized.

Meanwhile, a weird-looking creature creeped up and hopped down the table and into the left pocket of the journalist's green jacket, unseen.

"This, you see, is my passion, my personal project. This is who I am. We educate many young minds among these walls, and many old ones, too. In any normal day this place teems with people. Today however the library is empty and lifeless: everybody knew of your arrival, and people here don't care much for being photographed or filmed. We like our privacy, you know. Have I told you about our reading rooms yet?"

"Yes. Ten. You said you have ten."

"Actually, I said twelve. Come, come. I'll show you around."
The old man showed the reporter to the next room behind a glass door decorated with floral motifs.

"You really aren't short on nothing here, are you."

"Four and twenty work stations fully equipped with everything: computer, headphones, the whole shebang. And of course my favorite: pen, pencil and paper. I'm a nostalgic, you know. I couldn't live without them. Moreover, many people still use them. Actually, more than you'd think."

"And you've got ten reading rooms just like this one?"

"Well, no…"
"Ah-a! It was all too much already. Such valuable equipment in this place…"

"… it's twelve reading rooms. And this is nothing to the others. In fact, it's the smallest one. Don't fret, though, the other are nothing really humongous. The largest is equipped with barely less than a hundred workstations. Ninety-six, to be exact." said the old man with a huge smile on his face.
The reporter was dumbstruck. His mind couldn't wrap around the idea of a treasure that huge in a place so lost to the world, so disconnected from society, and moreover, kept in such a trivial wooden barrack, not even the largest, or at least the most noticeable in the Village.

"Did I spark your interest, lad?"

"Er. Well, yeah. I mean… this is really impressive, considering. However I am not sure a piece on a library is what my editor in chief had in mind when he sent me here, that's all."

"Not 'a library', young man, 'the' library! I'm sorry, what newspaper did you say you wrote for? I am old, you know, I forget things…"
"The Irish Times. As I was saying…"

"I can see your piece on the cover of tomorrow's issue already: 'An invaluable cultural patrimony hidden in the North of the Country.' How do you like it? Over two millions volumes, twelve fully equipped reading and studying rooms, and have I mentioned our collection of rare books, yet?"

"N-no, actually you haven't…" stuttered the journalist.

"Come, come! I bet it'll take your breath away." went on the old man, approaching what looked like the door to another room, but actually proved to be an elevator.

"I'm right behind you. Although, I'd like to take some pictures first?"

"Pictures? Didn't anybody tell you? We don't like being photographed."

"I didn't mean a picture of you. Just the library, maybe?"

"Don't worry about that. It'll be my pleasure to send you a couple of pictures to spice up your meager piece."

"M… meager? How dare you! It's two full columns, and on The Irish Times, for crying out loud! I wouldn't call it meager." the young reporter was too proud of his job at the newspaper to let that ancient know-it-all diminish it.

Meanwhile, the elevator reached the lowest underground floor.
"Yes, yes, of course. Your perfectly decent article, then. However, we're here now. Come. Come and see! Oh and I would like to point out for you readers that you, mr… mr… I'm sorry, it seems I've forgotten your name again. You, boy, are the first person to ever set foot in this room."

"James, James O'Dail. I'm honored, really. But weren't you just boasting about how this place is always 'teeming with people' at all hours?"

"I meant the first outsider. Usually only the villagers are allowed here. And now, look, how marvelous!" said the old man, dramatically opening the door to the room were the collection of rare and antique books was kept.

It was a dark room, the only illumination coming from a ceiling lamp projecting a low light on a stand, on top of which an old manuscript lay open. Its yellowy parchment pages were almost unreadable because of the old age and the advanced state of consumption of the paper. The reporter, speechless, advanced towards the stand, drawn in as from a magnet to the magnificent object showcasing in the middle of the room.

"Commendable acquisition, don't you think?"

Whilst the old man admired his temple, the bizarre little animal creeped out of the journalist's pocket, and begun it's descent towards the pavement. After long plotting and scheming it'd finally managed to sneak into that particular room, eluding all the

14

surveillance the old man had arranged to protect that place and the treasures stored in it.
"At a first glance, it would seem a very old artifact."

"It is the Diarmait Book, a work dating back to the VII century of the modern Era."

"Impossible! There's no such thing as the Diarmait Book, and even if there was one, it could never have ended up in a place such as this…"

"You asked your question, I gave you the answer. Either you decide to accept it, or the time hasn't come for us to come into the light yet."

Meanwhile the raterpillar was already feasting on a very scruffy looking manuscript, unfortunately left out of place, out of its protective case, by a clumsy novice. A less valuable copy of a french psalter, sitting on the floor next to a small wooden table in the darkest part of the room.

"Look old man, I know ancient texts and manuscripts like the back of my hands. I travelled all around Europe to study and consult them. I wrote my thesis on ancient manuscripts for crying out loud! This is not… what… Wait. Let me take a closer look!"

"No! Don't touch that. You can't touch it. Don't you see how delicate it is?"

"If that be the case, it would only deteriorate faster in a place like this. It needs a safe environment, constant temperature, absence of humidity…"

"You are absolutely correct. That is exactly the reason why this place is equipped with everything these babies need to ensure the best state of conservation."

"Don't be ridiculous, you couldn't possibly have the know-how."

The small creature curbing its appetite on the delicious page of the ancient french psalter was a pretty little thing, unknown to the outsiders but very well known and feared by the villagers, who worked really hard to keep the precious collection stored in the library out of its paws' reach. Its worm-like shape, the big pointy ears on its head, the four very tiny and agile legs it used to swiftly overcome any obstacle big or small, the tail at the end of its body and the unmistakeable color of its fur, changing from a dark grayish tone to a brownish one, didn't leave room for doubt. It was a raterpillar. And a very hungry one.

"Dear James, I regret to see that our interview has come to an end. I thought I was speaking to a mind truly open to knowledge, but I can see now how you suffer from the same disease affecting the rest of your people: that huge, throbbing vein, connecting your brain to other parts, carries in itself that disgusting, impalpable substance that's narrow-mindedness."

"Hold on a minute! Just who do you think you are, to talk to me like that! And I bet you don't even know the half of it. Well then, what say you of… of the Book of Kells? That, that is an old manuscript. A truly commendable acquisition, in your own words."

"James, you arrogant young man. From The Great Evangeliary of St. Columba, the original is currently part of the Trinity College's collection in Dublin, but we have a marvelous handcrafted reproduction right here.
Fourth case from the left, on your right. It should be dating back to the XII century."

"What? I never heard that a copy of that precious work was ever made… Ok then, let's say it exists and you have it. What is it even worth, compared to the surely more important Cathach of St. Columba?"

After gobbling up one corner of the psalter the raterpillar, reassured by the hassle occurring between its noisy companions of its being still unseen, took another piece of the precious book with its small rat-like paws and gulped it down in a split second. The old librarian even in the heat of the moment, couldn't ignore the tiny noise, and turned his gaze in search of the source. The raterpillar froze instantly, only recovering the use of its body and intellect after having made sure that the darkness and the parchment it was devouring were effectively hiding it from the old man's stare.

The two men resumed their quarreling:
"The Insular psalter from the VII century of the Royal Irish Academy Collection in Dublin? We have a reproduction here which contains pages lost even to the original manuscript. Though, lamentably, it appears our copy, too, lacks some of the original pages."

"You are a fool. There's no such thing as a copy of that manuscript in the whole wide world."

"If you believe so, I would encourage you to turn around and look. Third case on your left."
As he said the words, the old man pressed a button on a remote controller he kept in his robe, directing a light on the said manuscript.

"It can't be. What about Paulus Orosius, then?"

And it munched, and it crunched. The raterpillar had eaten so much by now, that it'd turned wobbly and sleepy. It was full, to the detriment of the psalter.

"We only have a XVI century copy of the Bobbio Orosius of the Ambrosian Library in Milan, also known as MS D 23 sup., written in VII century uncial."

"The Book of Durrow!"
"On your right, third volume on the left, third level." answered the old man, still worried about the noise he was sure he'd heard in the darkness. He could see it, the raterpillar, hidden in plain sight, attempting at the integrity of his treasure, now in terrible danger.

"The Northumbrian Gospel Book Fragment of Durahm."

"We keep two copies of that, one is in front of you, third level, yes, there. The other is in our laboratory, being prepped for the online auction we are hosting in a couple of months. Perhaps you'd be interested?"

"The Echternach Gospels, the Book of Lindisfarne…"

"Of course we keep them in our collection. And the most rare and precious copy of the Lichfield Gospels, as of today more often referred to as the St Chad Gospels or the Book of Chad, and two copies of the Codex Ardmachanus and…"

"And?"

"A manuscript, contemporary of the Codex Sangallensis, the St. Gall Gospel Book. The original is in Switzerland, as you may know, and consists of 134 pages. Ours has 144."

The young reporter, getting more frustrated and incredulous every minute, approached the impossibly rare book laying right in front of him. He could't bring himself to touch it, but thanks to his studies he could see even from a distance that it was indubitably an original.
A terribly rare, absolutely invaluable manuscript which couldn't possibly be left in such a place as that Village must be.

"What's going on? What are you doing here?"

From the shadows by the door, emerged the High Priestess of the Elm. Her disappointment towards the old librarian was more than eloquent in her features.

"Nothing. Nothing. Nothing to worry about." answered the old man.

"I believe we'll agree to disagree on the matter, dear. Mr O'Dail, I believe your work is finished, now. You will be escorted out of the Village."

"But. I. Actually…"

"I don't see why…"

"Nothing more to see, here. Isn't there, my dear? The interview is over. Mr O'Dail has all the information he needs to produce the groundbreaking piece of news I am confident he was sent here to write."

"Hold your horses now, miss…"

"I am asking you kindly, sir, to vacate the premises. You are no longer welcome here."

The old woman pointed her finger towards the elevator doors, where a young lad was already waiting for the reporter. James looked at the old librarian who couldn't but follow the woman's orders and show him out.
In the elevator, James apostrophized the kid.
"Isn't there anyone 'normal' in here? You. What is your name?"

"Lyon, sir. I'm afraid, though, I was ordered not to answer any more of your questions. To show you we mean no harm, however, it will be a young woman to escort you out of the Village, to your car."

Upon reaching the ground floor, they found the girl already waiting. She came by the guest's side, swift and silent as a shadow in the bright light of the sun. A shadow so beautiful, James was instantly stunned and jumped out of his skin when her chirping voice finally broke the silence.

"Good morning Mr. O'Dail. My name is Eleonor. Please, follow me."

James wouldn't utter another word. He followed her more than complacently. When they got out of the Village though, she left him at the edge of the small parking lot where the visitors were asked to leave their motors, the Village being an entirely no-motors area.

James mounted on the small rental, turned his keys, waved a clumsy goodbye and drove away towards Donegal, the town giving the name to the region Donegal on the beautiful coast of the Atlantic Ocean, from where he would take the train back to Dublin.

But he wasn't alone. A man was following him, under instructions from the High Priestess of the Elm to ensure his definitive arrival to the train station and into his seat on the train back to his hometown.

***

Upon his late arrival at the office, the Publishing House in Tara Street by the bridge on the Liffey, James had a long get-together with his editor in chief.

The man commissioned to his reporter a piece of news thoroughly concocted to inform the unaware reader of all that had really come to pass amongst those peasants, in the hideous Village in the North, and "leaving absolutely nothing to the imagination".

No one liked the people of the Village. No newspaper in Dublin had ever been soft, or even objective about them. On the contrary, it was the Irish tabloids the ones responsible for the Village's bad reputation: they were strangers, English for the most part, so they had to be different. For decades they had been portrayed in the tabloids as weirdos, dark, secluded, hundred percent full on batshit crazy people, living as savages in the North of the Country. Naturally by now the public believed the newspapers whenever the Village came up in the news associated to any and all sorts of nefarious things.

And even when something good about them came out, they became suddenly too perfect for that perfection not to be a façade behind which something rotten and wrong lay hidden. So it had to be, and so it was. At least for the general public whose mind had been since long molded into compliance through pieces of news written in a perfectly calibrated sympathy- and hatred-inducing tone.

But not all of it came from the inside: someone was inspiring, guiding, molding the information system as well as the public view. Someone schemed against the Village, hidden in the shadows.

***

The High Priestess of the Elm didn't beat around the bush and – presto – demanded an explanation of his husband, the High Priest of the Elm and Head Librarian of the Village.

"Was it really necessary to introduce the boy down here? What did you think he'd tell of what he saw? They'll say we are book thieves now, or worse, forgers!"

"But, my darling. You must believe that I didn't mean it to end like this. I just thought… If we showed our library…"

"I told you to be careful. I was against this whole newspaper idea from the beginning. I just hope… You didn't show… Did you?"

"Absolutely not. I didn't show him the Thirteenth Chamber. I didn't even mention it, not even once. Not even at all."

"When will you ever learn to protect yourself and all of us from your own ingenuity?" she muttered, sadly, hugging him.

Once his wife returned to her business, the High Priest began his hunt. He searched every corner of the room, confident he would discover the unmistakable traces of the tiny trespasser. And, blimey! When his blue-gray eyes met the unattended psalter in the corner of the room he knew that, once lifted the pages, he'd have found the sated raterpillar he was looking for.

"Bloody creeper! I'll teach you to ruin my books!"

He took the creature by its pink rat-like tail and put it in a box. Besides being a pillager of libraries and the scourge of librarians all over the globe, the raterpillar was actually a very useful and precious companion to them – once properly trained and under their careful control, of course – as its food preferences could be used to detect authentic manuscripts from fake modern reproductions. Its gluttony made easily detectable once a piece of sheepskin or goatskin parchment, vellum or even papyrus got in its smelling distance. It wouldn't look at linen twice, but it would become sleepy and doze off on hundred-percent pure silk covers. This little Attila would save the High Priest a lot of money of expensive professional bibliographer's advices.

The next day, with his breakfast, Eleonor brought the High Priest the day's newspapers. On the Irish Times' left column of the front page he found the article about the Village, though the title wasn't exactly the one he had anticipated.

"CHRONICLES OF A MIRACULOUS ESCAPE – our correspondent barely escapes with his life from a close encounter with the tribe of pseudo-Celts of the Village in the North."

The article portrayed, in a biting journalism lingo, the people of the Village as uncivilized savages and the High Priest of the Elm as an old senile almost illiterate dullard, who was supposed to divert with his gibberish the journalist's attention from the really scandalous piece of news concerning the Village: the black market trough very fishy online auctions of stolen rare and ancient manuscripts and substandard forgeries handcrafted in what the savages called "the Village's library".
The newspaper's deprecative intentions towards the Village were clear as day even in James' versions of the smallest facts. The green, sustainable no-motors policy of the Village became a ploy against the authorities, hampered in the exercise of their public mandates and an active discrimination against the disabled, all to keep under control the spreading of who knows how many terrible secrets. Of course he completely forgot to mention the horse-driven carriage service provided by the Village especially for the disabled. The piece ended with a call to action: the authorities should inspect the business

going on around the library and the librarian which, according to the reporter findings, had to be extremely suspicious.

The High Priest repined at the blatant lies and brash comments of the young journalist, whilst his wife's mood got darker and darker.

"Very nice indeed." exclaimed her when her patience – and the article – ended. "Next time, invite them for lunch, so they can write we're a cannibalistic tribe as well."

"That was in the Irish Independent two weeks ago, Ma'm." commented a young novice in an innocent tone.

***

That night on the way home James was lost in thoughts of fame and glory. His piece had made the front page of the newspaper, maybe one of these days he would be able to convince the editor in chief to publish his masterpiece on the unexplainable disappearance of VHS rentals…

He entered his home in the pink building at 11, Drumcondra Road Lower. Shut the door behind him and went for the light switch, but the light wouldn't come.

"The damned electricity is off again!" he exclaimed. Took his smartphone from his pants' pocket to switch on the torch app but a shadow moved in the dark, making him jump out of his skin and take four steps back. Suddenly, he was on the floor.

"Good evening, Mr O'Dail. I'm really sorry to disturb you like this, however a topic of the most urgent nature came to my attention, and I couldn't possibly leave it unattended. You see, the contents of the article you wrote is a huge lie. You know it, I know it, and your editor knows it as well. This bad information circle against the Village and the people in it has to stop. They haven't harmed you in any way. Just because they live differently it doesn't give you the freedom to speak so ill of them."

"Who are you? What are you doing in my house? I'll call the police!" shouted James, who was beginning to be afraid.

"I came here to deliver this letter. It is addressed to your editor in chief, and I'm sure you will pass it on to him, won't you? Oh and make sure you give him an account of our somewhat unpleasant meeting, as you give him my courtesies."

The man approached James looking right into his eyes, as if to evaluate him, then snapped:
"I cannot believe the mess your brain is. Straighten your facts and behave, I'll be watching you."

That said, he placed his hand on James' face making him fall asleep, helped him down on the pavement next to the door and left the apartment, vanishing in the darkness.

Next morning at dawn, James regained his senses. He felt dizzy and weird, as if images from a dark dream were spinning into his head and he just couldn't grasp them. Dismissing the feeling as the vestiges of a nightmare he surely didn't care enough to remember, he got up from the floor, realizing where he was laying and what he was wearing. He still had yesterday's clothes on, all wrinkled from the rough night on the floor. He got up, stretching painfully and as he straightened his back he felt something falling on the ground.
A closed envelope.
James called the police.

"Hello? Good morning, it's James O'Dail, I telephoned to call in a home intrusion…" soon, a police patrol car was parking in front of his building.

"Once again, from the top: yesterday at 8:00 PM you entered your apartment, the light didn't work and suddenly a man was there, menacing you."

"Yes."

"Could you give me a description of your aggressor?"

"It was dark. I couldn't see him."
 "But you knew he was a man."

"He spoke in a man's voice."

"And what did he say exactly?"

"He said… hold on a second… He said, he wanted me to deliver this envelope. To my editor in chief. My boss." he said, showing the envelope to the policeman.

"This?" the policeman opened the letter and briefly read its content. Then passed it on to his colleague and went on with the reconstruction. "And what did he say to "menace" you?"

"Well… he said… he menaced… he said to deliver the letter."

"Ok. But what about the menacing part?"

"Listen, I don't think it's not menacing to enter in your own house and find a stranger in the dark. Do you?"

"Of course. That is, if this is what actually happened. Couldn't you have opened the door to this 'stranger' yourself?"

"Of course not!"

"Did he break a window? Do you have a backdoor?"

"No. No backdoor, no broken windows."

"Maybe then you left a window open and he came in from there?"

"No, no. Not possible. I'm sure…"

"Mr. O'Dail. There's no sign of a break-in here. The lock is not broken or scratched or anything else. The only way someone could have entered here is with a pair of keys."
 "A passepartout, maybe?"

"Sir, these new locks are passepartout proofed, he must have used regular keys. How many copies do you have and where do you keep them? Are they all accounted for? Did you even check?"

"Of course I have! There are three copies. One I have, another is at my fiancee's house – she had it when I called her to check. The spare is on a key-hook just next to the entrance."

"This one?" intervened the other agent pointing to the key hanging next to the door.

"That one."

"Let's give this a try." the policeman closed and opened the door with the keys.

"I don't understand." James was getting confused again.

"Are you sure your fiancee's copy is accounted for?"

"Yes, yes. I'm sure. As I told you, I called her sooner this morning and she said she had it in her handbag."

"Look, we don't have time to waist here. As I see it, yesterday night you got a bit drunk, then this 'stranger' knocked on you door and gave you the envelope. He left and you passed out on the floor and had a nightmare."

"I'm telling you, I wasn't drunk! I am not confused! He... I remember him now. He had blue eyes!"

"Mr. O'Dail! You told me it was so dark you couldn't see your attacker, and now you are telling me he had blue eyes? And you'll insist you weren't drunk, now, too. You haven't driven your car in that state, have you?" the policeman said, in a somewhat menacing tone. That story was getting more and more absurd.

"No! No. I wasn't drunk! I wasn't!"

"Just listen to me, now. Take a good long hot shower, pop a pill and take a nap. You'll see that, when you wake up all refreshed, you'll remember it just as I told you. In any case, our work here is done. There's no elements sustaining a break in nor the presence of a stranger in your house, and no description for a suspect hunt. You wouldn't have us stop every man with blue eyes on the streets, wouldn't you now?"

The policemen left the house making jokes about the loser who drunk too much and didn't even care for the volume of their voices.
James locked the door and went to take a quick shower before leaving for work. He was late, again.

"Good morning chief."

"Good morning O'Dail, late again, I see."

"I am sorry, there was a mishap…"

"Oh, really? What then?"

"Yesternight a man broke into my house to give me this for you and warn me that he will be watching me. He said something about the newspaper article…"

"Did you call the police?" the editor in chief took the envelope – now open – with a sour expression, then gnawed a little harder on his cigar's butt.

"I called them, they came, saw and left, saying there was 'no sign of break in'. I can't wrap my head around it, I am sure he didn't have the keys."

"Looks like the perfect piece for page 7…"

"Of course I thought so, too. However…"

"However?" the editor in chief took the cigar out the corner of his mouth to spit the chewed tobacco in the bin under the desk.

"Police went away empty handed. People would think I'm the regular nut-job."

"Right. The police… well, they read the letter. Let's see if we can get anything from here." he opened the envelope and read the letter. His face kept getting darker and darker while he progressed. He stood up, then sat back down, looking at the young journalist in front of him.
"James, forget this story. Today you are writing a piece on degradation of the suburbs north-west of Dublin. Go to Ballymoon and stay there until you've got something for me."

"But… what about the letter?"

"What letter? Nothing that concerns you. It was addressed to me, after all… Are you still here? Go on, lad. Go on."

James left closing the door behind his back, the editor in chief was already on the phone.

"Good morning, I received a letter, it is paramount that I speak to… Oh, it's you… did you receive one, too? Oh. I am sorry. No. Yes, of course. No more articles. No. Well, yes but I couldn't have imagined… yes, of course. I understand. Of course. I'm sorry. I will make things up… Oh. So, I won't, no. Yes, no, of course, you're right, as usual. Silence… Silence is golden. Of course. I'm sorry for

the hindrance… The journalist? No, I will take care of him. No, he wont. He'll stay here in Dublin, for a while. Thank you. Again. Good… Goodbye."
Once the line died on the call, the editor ripped the letter to confetti, then threw the pieces of paper in the bin and vented out his frustration on the objects laying on his desk. "Damn you dogs sons of bitches! You'll pay for everything. Bastards! I'll make you pay!"

Rubbing a black and red skull with yellow eyes, symbol of the Skulls of York gang, he had tattooed on the inside of his left wrist, he took the phone once again and punched in a number, as fast as he could.

"Hallo. It's me. Pass me on to the Boss. Yes. Yes. Good morning. Yes, it's worse than we imagined. They have spies everywhere and their influence… it's just as you suspected. I just received a letter from the man with the blue eyes… yes, their 'guardian angel'. I don't know… he menaced the writer of the article, the police read the letter and wouldn't even take the statement… next article, he says, he gets me kicked out of the newspaper. And he menaced the chief here, too. He said they're pulling the fundings… I know whom our biggest financier is, but I wasn't aware… Who could have thought they'd be in the shade of the giant… That's it. How can I be calm now? I need reinforcements. No… No I won't take initiatives. I'll wait for your instructions. Just…

we need to speed things up here, or we're going to succumb… ok. No, ok. I'm sorry. You are right Boss. No rush actions against them. I'm just worried… ok, I'll wait for them. Thank you. Thank you, bye."

***

"Good morning old man, sorry to bother. I was looking for the High Priest…"

"Of the Elm? You're lucky! You just found him. Did we have an appointment?"

"Oh, it's you? Vey well, yes. The name is Corrige, Antony."

"Corrige as Patrick and Alicia Corrige, I suppose?"

"Yes, it's me. I came here to ask some information about you summer camp for my kids…"
"I'm here to help you with whatever information you may be interested in. But fist could I ask who recommended us to you?"

"Mr. Tyrrel. He sent his three kids here last summer."

"Freddy, Pat and Leila. Yes, I remember them. The three typhoons…"

"Indeed they are, but after their stay here… they came home so changed…"

"Did they, really?"

"A good change, of course. An improvement, really."

"Yes, yes. We worked very hard with those three. Brilliant kids, really. They're coming back this summer, you know?"

"That is why I thought that maybe… Maybe this year my kids could come, too."
 "Are you from London as well?"
 "Yes."

"And you made all this way just for this? We could have spoken via web!"

"Well, er… I was in Londonderry for work and so… I thought… you know, there's some things that are better spoken eye to eye… eheheh."

"Very well, then. Let's talk about the reason you are actually here, now. Your kids, how old are they?"

"Didn't you receive my e-mail?"

"Yes, but wouldn't it be easier if we just talked?"

"Yes, of course. I didn't mean… I just meant that I sent you all the information about the kids."

"Of course, very well. So, how old are they?"

"Patrick is ten, Alicia eight."
"She is a bit young, but I am sure with some proper fore-training our novices will be able to spend some quality time here with her and of course have fun. The camp will be good for her as well as for her brother, I'm sure. Your kids will be in the best hands. Is that all?" asked the old man, prompting the other to talk. He was sure the greatest issue hadn't been addressed yet.

"Well… how do I put it… I saw only extremely good reviews of your camp – besides the recommendation of the Tyrrels, I mean."

"Antony, what exactly is it you're worrying about?"

"Look… I don't know… I'm not sure…"

"Let me help you. Might it have something to do with religion?"

"Well… yes. Actually, that's the main concern."

"What creed?"

 "Anglican, of course."

"Very well. We have a Pastor in our Village, you know?"

"Do you, really?"

"Of course. Why the face?"

42

"I… I thought… maybe… I mean, you…"

"What about us? You thought we would spend the summer indoctrinating the children? What exactly did Mr. Tyrrel tell you about us?"

"Nothing, really. Nothing bad. He said he was extremely satisfied of your work with his children. Actually it's not me, who's worried… you know how it is."

"You wife, perhaps? Does she worry about the children's creed? And she asked you to come here and see for yourself that there's nothing going on here.
It's perfectly understandable, of course the mother should and must be informed of what the children will be doing here. And you, too. We can see how concerned you are in regards to your kids' education and well being. But tell me, are they as lively as the Tyrrels?"

"No, no. Of course not. Well, Patrick tends to be a little hyperactive, whilst Alicia is quite shy. Nothing out of the ordinary, though. The other reason I'm here is more of a personal curiosity. I was wandering, how did you manage to accomplish all this, starting with nothing but the land… you are a well adjusted community now, and it's been what, a couple of decades?"

"You see, Anthony, it's a fascinating story. Everything started, as you said, some decades ago. The society of the industrial revolution was in a sharp decline, and people begun to understand the importance of a change. We all struggled with the need to conduct a greener, more sustainable way of living. Only after a while people started to notice us, but even earlier, those few who believed in the same dream, who shared the same vision, had already embarked on our journey. What separates us from the rest of the world is the consciousness that the Earth is a living being, just like us, which is something the majority of people isn't aware of, just because you know, she doesn't walk or breathe like us. But as a matter of fact, she does, just, in a different way. And if she didn't we wouldn't, either. She is the Great Mother to us. Not religiously, as many people erroneously think. To us it's a fact. A physical, concrete, tangible, reasonable fact." the High Priest of the Elm took a handful of dirt from the ground and delicately scattered it back in the air. "It feeds us, quenches our thirst, offers us protection. And the Sun? It is an astral object, of course. But if he weren't there, where would we be? What would become of us without him? He's not only a concept, an abstraction to adore and mindlessly put on a pedestal. I don't adore him, I love him as a Father in the sky. A real father, a concrete, tangible physical presence looking over us, warming us up, procuring us food and company with his light. There's nothing absurd or mischievous in this. It is, in fact, the simplest more natural truth. It may come as a shock to you, but here, in the Village, no one will ask you what you believe in, if you pray your God on Saturday, Sunday or any other day of the week, how many times every day and in what language, if it is a humanoid being or a disembodied philosophical or linguistic concept. Here you can believe or not, and if you do, no one is going to tell you in what deity to put your trust. After all, no God would ever discourage a human being to love God, so why should I, how could I? Why – if they even are two distinct beings and not just two manifestations of the same energy – should my God be better than yours? Believe me, whomever here loves a God, will always be accept from Him for that love, no matter His name. So maybe, in the end, we can just be all on the same side. Names may differ, rites may differ, but we love our Gods and it is all that matters. Being Celts is also about this, live and let live, be free to be whoever you are, however you are, and let the others benefit of the same rightful freedom. Of course we try to make a good use of that freedom and our time, we follow our festivities and of course we worship those beings that let us be who we are. But that doesn't automatically entail that every other way of life must be condemned. We believe in a God, after all. A universal God who created everything, who generated the first spark of what became the Universe with all the seeable and unseeable things.

We love and give thanks to our Earth and Sun for all they give us, and by doing so, we ultimately give thanks to that same God which created us and them. For if he hadn't created our Great Mother and our Great Father to feed and guide and protect and warm us, we must know that we wouldn't be here now. But am I boring you? Am I too repetitive?"

"Not at all. You see, something you said… I didn't expect… I am grateful. Thank you."

"The light in your eyes tells me you felt something for what I said, I'm glad. Would you like some tea?"

"Yes, thank you. But you were saying…"

"Of course even the spirits of the Celts can be different from one-another. After long decades of struggle we decided to create a community on these lands, with whomever of the Celts would decide to embrace our vision and work with us to make it prosper. We met in Duncarron, another traditional Village in the outskirts of Edinburgh. Have you heard its name before?"

"Yes, I think I heard of it."

"They came from everywhere. The North of France, Lyone, Marseille, Hamburg, Bern, Villach, Bardi, the eastern Europe, the Hiberic Peninsula – both from Spain and even a small congregation based in Portugal – from Scandinavia, St. Peterburg, Kiev, the Middle East, China, Australia, Americas. There were hundreds, thousands even. A festive melting pot. We drunk, we sung, we discussed, and in the end we came up divided in two major factions. One believes that the Celtic culture, as inseparable and essential part of our world, must and should naturally evolve with the course of our lives. Those who recognized themselves in this precept are those who came here and build this Village, this community, or stayed behind and named us as the rightful custodians of this way of living, which emulates that of our ancestors."

"And what about the other faction?"

"The Skull's. Well, we are malleable, but they… they don't believe in any kind of improvement or change which may interfere with the Celts' original way of life. They practice the cult as they believed it was except, because our culture always had an oral form of transmission, the only written accounts of our traditions were made from outsiders, and we could never be sure of their accuracy or veracity. Still, they insist they are the true Celts. Their headquarters are in York."

The old man seemed unstoppable, it had been some time since someone had really listened to what he had to say. And he seemed to never run out of new, interesting information.

"You see, Antony, since the dawn of time in every land people alternated with other people, cultures with other cultures: Assyrians, Babylonians, Hittites, Phoenicians, Etruscans, all these people were eventually succeeded by others in their own lands and their cultures disappeared. Why then did we survive? Of course Greeks, Romans, Egyptians have survived the trial of time, adapting and leaving behind texts and architecture, keeping alive the track of their passage. The Celts left no records of themselves behind, not one bit of information that may give us a unitary cultural identity, nothing survived our ancestors, but for some partial recollections compiled by their contemporaries. Nonetheless we thrive. And you know why? Being a Celt isn't just being part of a culture, some artificial societal bond made by man. Celts are humans, and animals, and plants, trees, and crystals and stones, souls and spirits, the ground we walk on, the water in rivers and springs, the air we breathe. Many things have passed, some people subjugated us, some tried to exterminate us, some to turn us into something we weren't or annihilate us into submission, but none of them succeeded. We never disappeared. Truth be told, we don't share a genetical bond with our ancestors. In my own veins runs more easily Indo-

European, Latin, Germanic, Viking, Asian, African blood, rather than Celtic. But blood matters nothing in comparison to this land. This land exudes the Celtic spirit from every pore. It is impossible not to let it permeate us and be swayed, loved, and let ourselves love and live like the old inhabitants of this land. No God would destroy us, no man in the name of no God managed to accomplish that. I believe in a superior entity, and I believe it wants us to go on existing. Think about it. Maybe there is a secret indelible pact between God and us, and maybe thanks to it we still exist on this same land which saw our culture be born. God loves this land, our land, loves those who inhabit them and, let me tell you one last thing, he wants us to be exactly the way we are supposed to be, according to our own culture."

"Wonderful. Sensational. You… you!"

"Oh, come on. After all, I didn't really say nothing special."

"Do you have a summer camp for adults, too?"

"Of course. Would you be interested?"
"Yes, yes I would! Of course, I must speak first with my wife, but if she agrees, maybe we could come here together, the four of us, to spend summer here!"

"Well, you know, our summer camps are a place for study, not exactly the ideal vacation place."

"Just as I imagined. Work and study!"

"And a little bit of fun, of course."

"If everything goes according to plans, how do I make a reservation?"

"By phone call or email, as you prefer. The summer camp is limited number, though. If you really wish to spend some time with us this summer I would recommend you make your reservation within the week."

"Duly noted. I will call Friday at the latest to confirm or delete the reservation. Could I ask you one last thing, though. That sign there, I can see the word "library" on it, translated in many languages all of which I can at least recognize. All, but one. The last one at the bottom of the list, right after Chinese and Japanese. Which language is that?"

"What sign are you talking about?" asked the High Priest, surprised.

“Last one on the left. There.”

“That? Oh, that is ancient Gaelic.” answered the old man trying to stay calm.

Antony Corrige wasn’t supposed to see the sign at all. He wasn’t one of them, or was he? He saw the sign, so he must be a true Celt, even though he probably didn’t know it yet. The High Priest begun wandering where the man could ever have come from.
Wherever that was, he was sure to have found a brother.

End of the Pilot

Episode 01
The HERBARIUM

"That's interesting. You have classes of ancient Gaelic in the summer program?"

"Classes, you say? Well, we mostly use this language for rituals and such, but only for its traditional value. Truth be told, it is a dead language. But if you really mean to learn it, we may be able to arrange something for you. It won't be easy, though. You'll have to study hard," answered the High Priest of the Elm, still unsettled. The man in front of him was, in fact, a long-lost brother of the Celts and, by the look of it, he was totally unaware of this truth.

"That's fantastic! I can't wait to tell my children!"
"First of all, you should talk things through with your wife. She might not be so happy about your idea of spending holidays here with us."

"You're right, of course. Tell me, how would you tell her, if you were in my shoes and you really – really wanted to convince her?"

"Honestly, I have no idea. After all, I'm not in your shoes. I've never even met her!"

"Well... she won't bite. Although, I have to say she's a bit anxious and reluctant towards trying new things. She won't change her habits, her opinions are set in stone, and she'll oppose to whatever I say – because she's always right and I never, of course. And if, by chance, I ever were right, she'll say that whatever I said was her opinion since the beginning and if only I had listened to her and done as she'd said…"

"Come, now, I wouldn't take it so far. It's your own wife you're talking about."

"Of course, you're right. I'm not exaggerating, though. But for sure you must know better: women are all alike."
"I understand your need to vent out, Antony. However, I would encourage you to see reason on the matter: after all you're talking about human beings. There's no sense in generalization," answered the High Priest mildly. "Why don't you bring your wife to our open-day we're having in a couple of weeks or so? It might be a good opportunity to show her around and tell her about your idea for the summer."

"An open-day? Like at school?"

"Precisely. This way, I will get to know her and maybe we could try to convince her together. Would this weekend be good for you?"

While the two men went over the details of the appointment for the coming weekend, the High Priestess of the Elm was studying them from a distance, a disapproving look in her eyes.

"There he is, my husband the procrastinator. How does he do that: every time I need him for something, he'll manage to disappear into thin air, and go play with his books or make new friends…"
"I'm done here, do you need something else of me before I go?" asked a young priestess.

"Oh Annah, just one more thing, if you may: go to my husband and kindly remind him that we have a job to do at the Herbarium. We are late for our appointment with the Great High Priestess already."

"Of course ma'am. And… the outsider?"

"Have Lyon escort him out of the Village. I believe he's got what he came for, by now, and my husband and I have yet a lot to accomplish before dinner."

The priestess followed her superior's orders and brought back the High Priest of the Elm to his consort. When he arrived, he didn't even give her the time to begin her reprimand.

"He's a brother!" exclaimed the man in a hushed agitated voice, bursting with excitement.

"Pray, what?" asked the High Priestess coming closer and moving her hair away from her ears to hear better.
"He is a brother of the Celts!" exclaimed him in a higher tone, as she jumped back with an annoyed look in her eyes.

"Why would you say so?"

"He's got the Sight."

"Are you sure?"

"Yes, yes! He saw the invisible language!"

"You're not trying to fool me again, are you?"

"No!"

"Why haven't you stopped him, then!"

"He's coming back in two weeks with his wife."

"Is she…"
"No. Well, I don't know yet. She's coming so she can take a look around before the family comes for the summer camp."

"So?"

"So, once the wife comes here, it's settled!"

"You always count the chickens before they hatch, my dear. However, I was looking for you because we have an appointment at the Herbarium. The Great High Priestess is waiting for us… oh, look, for fifteen minutes now. Get a move on, we're late."

"Right! The Herbarium. I almost forgot…" the High Priest played dumb, while his wife didn't know anymore whether to laugh in exasperation or cry in discomfort.

"You… You… You're unbelievable. Let's go now!"

The couple promptly left the house and went to the residence of the Great High Priestess, where an extremely annoyed, grumpy, elderly woman was waiting for them.

The group cut across the Village and passed over a small canal crossing a stone bridge that connected the side of the Village to the one where the Herbarium was.

They then took a gravel path across the outer fields of the Herbarium walking through progressively larger lots separated by plant variety. Finally, they reached a wooden door on the back of the Herbarium, a building where plants and herbs were grown and processed to serve the medical and nutritional needs of the Village.

Once inside, the group entered a decontamination chamber where sterilized sets of green suits, green rubber boots, white latex disposable gloves and masks and blue caps awaited them. Once everyone had their sterilized apparel on, the Great High Priestess punched in a security code and the three entered the laboratory, where a summit meeting awaited them.

The curator of the Herbarium greeted them coldly, irritated by their lateness.

"Good morning everyone. Any news?"

"Nothing new or, actually, no good news. The situation is getting worse."

In the past weeks, over a hundred plants had suffered unexplainable damages. Whatever it was, it was damaging them and arresting their growth and so close to harvest. At the beginning of the spring, the damage was circumscribed to the plants in the greenhouse, but as summer drew nearer, the plants grown in the crops outside had started to develop the same symptoms.

The Herbarium's collection counted more than 240 varieties of aromatic and medicinal plants. They were grown, harvested, selected, processed and blended into tablets, ointments, syrups, powders: medicines and panaceas for the people of the Village and the brothers of the Celts scattered around the world. Once harvested, the best aromatic plants were sent to the kitchen for the preservation or the preparation of meals. There was an agricultural section for crops, a forestry section for the repopulation of the endangered flora of the region, one for rare or endangered medicinal plants and one for the research of new and mysterious medicinal and aromatic plants.

One must have a knack for gardening and a profound knowledge of botany, agronomy, and phytopharmacy to preserve and grow that green treasure. Precisely for these reasons, Isabella Garcia had been chosen as the Head and curator of the Herbarium. She was an American agronomist from Wrightwood, a small mountain town in San Bernardino, California.

She didn't have the beauty of youth, but she was fascinating still with her deep gaze, her short hair, shaded in grey with strands of the same blond as when she was a girl still sparkling here and there. Wiccan priestess and fervent practitioner, she had left her home for her unconditional love of nature and had ended up in the Village, where she had lived ever since, well integrated into its Celtic community. She had taken on the task of creating and running the Herbarium of the Village because, at the time, it seemed impossible to succeed in the deed with the climate and terrain typical of that part of Ireland.

Stubborn and meticulous, she had finally succeeded. Also, thanks to the help and involvement of a workforce of almost twenty people every day, only twelve of which possessed the necessary qualifications and competencies and had a full job with her at the Herbarium. Six more people every day were employed in the crops, a hard work that every unspecialised worker of the Village alternated daily with other less demanding tasks necessary to the maintenance of the Village.

In the end, thanks to the Great Mother, Isabella had managed to produce on those lands all the plants necessary to meet all of the Village's demands. Two-hundred-and-forty classified, certified, fortified and improved plants: a real treasure had come out of her expert hands.

Of course, she had faced many difficulties, failed many experiments and still had a long way to go with her improvements but this terrible mess – almost certainly caused by some resilient parasites – had stopped the progress of her work and needed to be addressed and resolved at once.

***

James couldn't understand what was going on those days. He felt persecuted, as if someone was following him around, watching his every move. At last, he became depressed and paranoid. Especially coming home at night was a nightmare. As soon as he stepped in, with a hand still holding the door open, he would try the light. If it worked, once closed and secured the door, he would search each and every room of the house. First, he would look into the storage room and the closet and even behind the pantry doors – as if anyone but a dwarf or a very small child could even fit in such a narrow space. Then he would move on to the bedroom. He would turn on the light from the small corridor that separated the living room from the rest of the apartment. He'd stretch his arm out in the dark room, then, as the light came on, he would immediately throw himself on the ground to check under the bed. Then he would slam open all the doors of the wardrobe, to take by surprise any unwanted hidden guest. He didn't think that, if anything, that was the best way to actually end up overpowered by an assailant. Finally, he would check the small bathroom – where only a fool would think of hiding: the shower box had transparent plastic shower tents, there was no hiding space behind the opened door, and the only walkable space in the room was a teeny tiny crack between the toilet and the sink, which offered no kind of cover.

Once the apartment was thoroughly inspected, James would return to the living room, sit on the large sofa – taking another long, searching look underneath it first – and stiffly sit there in absolute silence listening for any little noise that might alert him of a presence in the house. During those moments of unjustified fear and paranoia, strings of questions came to his mind: who was the man with blue eyes? Why had the editor in chief behaved how he had, upon hearing him mentioned? Who were really the people of the Village? How could they be in possession of invaluable treasures, such as any library in the world would want to have in their vaults? James needed answers to these questions. He thought he'd made a try with his editor in chief first, who seemed to know more than he'd shared. But how to approach him? An interrogation in the workplace was out of the question. James felt he should try to meet him outside the office, as for a fortuitous coincidence, and then maybe invite him for a drink and take the opportunity to find out something more about that mysterious letter. He switched off his cellphone to charge it and opened the fridge, finally at ease, to prepare some dinner.

***

"This is the ginger we harvested this morning. Look!" exclaimed Isabella, the curator of the Herbarium, showing off the battered remains of the rhizome. "It's irrecoverable. And look at this Jerusalem artichoke: there's almost nothing left of it," she added, handing over the mangled root.

"Is this only affecting tubers and roots?" asked then the Great High Priestess.

"At first we thought so, too. In fact, we hoped that be the case. Unfortunately, however, the problem appears to be more serious," replied the deputy curator showing three other plants. "This rosemary is the fourth plant in two weeks that we found completely dried up overnight. Half this season's harvest of hypericum flowers did not even blossom. Our lemongrass was ravaged…"

"And you have no idea of what could be causing all this?"

"Not at all. That's why we called you. If it's an animal, parasite, insect, microbe or infesting bacteria, it's none I've ever encountered. And it is definitely not the terrain, nor anything in it. We always check every little detail, analyse each different phase of our work and report everything in our records. Each plant has its own protocol from seed to harvest to the selection of the new seeds for the next sowing. I checked and re-checked our records for this batch and everything is right on schedule… except for the plants!" Isabella ranted out, visibly frustrated.

"What about the plants from the Sacred Wood?" asked the Great High Priestess worriedly.

"Those were left untouched. Nothing wrong with the magical plants. Until now, that is."

"Well, well, well. This makes me think that maybe…"

"Did you just have an idea?" the High Priestess of the Elm looked at her husband, knowing that hc had thought of something and was now lost in his thoughts.

"Since whatever it is, it does not touch the magical plants… It must be something that comes from the Sacred Wood."

"We cannot be sure yet. After all, at first the problem seemed to concern only a limited number of plants, but it is expanding now," the curator was still doubtful.

"Of course, of course. Very well. I will need to go over some of my books. You continue your field study and I'll go back to the library if that's all?"

"Any useful information will be welcomed news." replied the deputy, but the High Priest of the Elm was already leaving the laboratory.

"Just another perfect excuse to go burrow himself in his beloved library. He will die in there." complained the High Priestess of the Elm who, practical woman that she was, would rather have found a solution by looking at the actual plants.

"Have you read the papers today?" asked Annah then, addressing the Great High Priestess.

"I did not have the time yet. Is there anything of interest?" asked her, still distracted by the Herbarium's situation.

"In the local section of The Times, there's serious news concerning one of our former sisters."

"Who?"

The Great High Priestess could feel a tempest approaching.

***

As soon as the High Priest of the Elm entered the library, he was welcomed by the insistent ring of the phone.
"Kids! Anyone? Why no one ever picks up the damn phone…" he complained, finally reaching out to take the call:
"Hello?"

"Good morning. Have you read the article in the Irish Times?"

"Yes. I really don't understand why that journalist would write such nonsensical…"

"I don't either, but now we have a bigger problem. The content of the article, gibber as it was, was taken pretty seriously by the Minister for Culture, Heritage and the Gaeltacht. From the information I received, Government inspectors will be sent your way to assess the value and the ownership rightfulness of the cultural patrimony in your possession. They will want answers concerning your books, answers on where did they come from, or how did you pay for them, all your tax records and other such things…"

"Oh well, that I really did not expect. We have all the paperwork here, somewhere. Let me just… I will ask Leon to help find and collect all the papers we need before their arrival."
"I don't want to get you worried, but be wary: they are moving weirdly fast, I'm sure they will do anything to get their hands on your books. Call John and Terence, it can't hurt to have a couple of lawyers at your sleeve on this occasion, just to be sure no one can take anything away from the library. You understand, don't you?"

"Sure. I will do as you say. Thanks, Hubert. Thank you."

"My pleasure," replied the man, ending the conversation and the call.

***

The moment James switched his cell phone back on, he found that he had received a lot of calls, messages, video messages and so on. But only one thing really worried him: thirty-seven unanswered calls had come from the newspaper landline, a dozen more from a couple of numbers he did not recognize and about twenty from the mobile of his editor in chief, whom he called back immediately without wasting another second.

"Where the hell have you been? We have been calling all day! Government officials were here this morning, they requisitioned all your notes from your article about the Village and now they are looking for you. They said they need to ask you some questions. They also left their contact with me: you must call them as soon as possible."

"I am sorry, boss, I switched off the phone to recharge it."

"What are you, idiot? Do I really need to tell you that a true reporter never – ever – switches off his mobile? You were minding your own business, weren't you? Look, I don't even want to know. Fix this. Right now. I don't want no more of those Gov. Op. faces in my office, is that clear?"

"Very. I'll call them first thing in the morning," answered James, cringing.

***

The Great High Priestess returned to her home accompanied by her deputy, the High Priestess of the Elm. Once inside, they rushed to the computer and opened The Times' website at the page of the local news.

"Camden! There she was," the women weren't really concerned about the news so much as of finding out the whereabouts of their long-lost sister. Then, the title of the piece caught their attention.

"Great Goddess! What was predicted is coming true. This must be the obscure event we foresaw in last year's predictions. I sure hoped, just for this once, the seers were mistaken but since the predictions are true, terrible days await us."

"We must intervene. The seers were clear: if we don't do something the future will become even darker," the priestesses looked worriedly at one another. The time for a difficult choice was fast approaching.

"What are we going to do?" the Great High Priestess stood silently in deep thought, musing over all the possible solutions, then gave her instructions to her deputy in chief.

"Do not share this information with anyone, at least until next week. This shall grant me enough time to think and pray, I'll ask the Goddess and maybe I will find a solution. I will need the deepest concentration. Cancel all my personal appointments and cover for me as best you can. If anyone asks, I am not well. My old age will make it a good enough excuse."

The High Priestess of the Elm nodded. She'd make arrangements for the orders of his superior to be carried out, ensuring the quiet concentration necessary for the matriarch to pray, fast and seek the Great Goddess' answers.

A few days passed and the High Priest of the Elm, having completely wiped out of his mind Hubert's phone call, went back to the Herbarium. He'd spent hours and hours studying his manuscripts and, finally, he believed he had found out who the infesting parasite responsible for the devastation of the plants was.

The High Priest was so excited about the news, that he forgot to wear his sterilized scrubs, thus provoking Isabella's immediate rebuke: "High Priest! Out! Seriously! Can you even read at all?" she shouted, ushering him out and pointing to the huge red and white sign inviting all visitors to wear the sterilized clothing before entering the laboratory.

Blushing at the unexpected reprimand, the High Priest apologized and run out to get changed. When he came back wearing the scrubs, the curator's face still looked pretty annoyed. He apologized again and tried to distract her with his great news.

"I haven't found the solution to the problem yet… but I think I know what will!"

Isabella, doubtful but intrigued, turned her face slightly towards him, as her deputy already hung from the lips of the wise old man.
"Could you tell me whether the plants from the Sacred Wood are still uncontaminated?"

"Yes. They grow luxuriant just as always." the deputy answered holding his breath.

"Very good, very good. Well, according to my research, each infesting parasite selects its food based on nutritional needs, but no regular parasite makes a distinction based on the plants being
magical or non-magical. Therefore the parasite we are looking for must be magical in origins, so we

may infer it must have wandered here from the Sacred Wood."

"So what creature do you think it is?"

"Lamentably, I'm not sure yet. You wouldn't give me enough time for a prolonged observation of their nutritional habits, and there are various hypotheses amongst both animals and insects that could be the culprit of this devastation, not to mention the even more fascinating possibility of them being a combination of more than one of these pretty little creatures," said the High Priest of the Elm smiling satisfied with his research and excited to help capture and maybe even study what could be an exotic creature from the Sacred Wood.

"So we're back to the start again," the deputy exclaimed distracted, trying to hide a lock of red hair back under his cap. The director was glaring at him, she knew he would not remember to change his gloves, now contaminated by his hair.

"Not exactly. You see, the guardians of the Sacred Wood breed a creature that they use as an observer. A creature that can recognize and keep under control all the magical creatures of the Sacred Wood. That's what is going to help us: the hawk-a-mole!" the High

Priest proudly showed to Isabella and her deputy an ancient book, open to the page where the extravagant animal was depicted.

"The hawk-a-what?" exclaimed the deputy, rubbing his nose with his other gloved hand. Isabella was about to lash out for all the sterilization-protocol breeching that was being performed in front of her, and by a scientist of all people.

"Hawk-a-mole. A cute small bird, about as big as my hand. It has soft black feathers with brown hues, the sharpest eyesight, an extraordinary sense of smell and mole-like paws, which are perfect to dig out his favourite meal from the ground. He favours earthworms, larvae, and small infesting rodents. Its small curved beak is extremely hard, and can be a deadly weapon."

"And… where do we find one?"

"As I told you, Breton and Arkon use them to patrol the Sacred Wood and the Haunted Forest. We will ask them one for a temporary loan."

"Are you sure they'll let you take one? Knowing how possessive, how proprietary they are…" the curator wasn't yet sold on the High Priest's solution.

"Tomorrow morning I will go there myself and ask for the loan. I won't let you down. I will return with this lovely creature and I'm sure, with its help we will solve the mystery, you'll see."

"I wonder how an animal of the Sacred Wood could possibly have arrived in here," mused Isabella, openly glaring at her deputy who was now insistently scratching a very red and swollen left ear.

"I have no idea. But as you said if it were anything else, you'd have found and solved the problem already."

"All right. We are totally in the dark anyway, let's see if this hawk-a-mole can help us," after all, thought the curator escorting the two sanitary hazardous men out of her laboratory, there didn't seem to be any other alternative solution to the disastrous devastation that was threatening her treasured Herbarium.
As soon as they left the laboratory, the High Priest turned to face the deputy.

"You know, my dear friend, your left ear is swelling dramatically. I would go have it looked at if I were you."

"It stings… I cannot help myself… I must scratch it! It's terrible!"

"If you keep scratching it like that, it will either fall off or swell up bigger than your face. Follow my advice, just go to the doctor."

***

A morning with the Government inspectors left James exhausted. The Gov. Op.s had spent hours grilling him about the Library of the Village, its collection and the collocation of each manuscript in the various chambers of the building. Nonetheless, James decided to pursue his intention of casually bumping into his editor in chief after work. He had been stalking the man for some days and by now he knew his habits well enough to be able to casually find himself in the right place at the right time to meet him. It did not take long for the ideal scenario to come up. The editor was a true man of habit: every evening at the exact same time he would leave the office to go for a beer at the usual place, the Viking pub 'The Long Stone' on Townsend Street, a few blocks from where the newspaper offices used to be. Tourists came to see the pub from all over the globe as though that building was some sort of attraction, rustic and traditional with its exposed bricks, the summer garden in the courtyard and the medieval-style battlements on its walls. The windows showcased light brown wood interiors in a traditional but still elegant style, a perfect setting to expose ancient books, old bottles and other objects of the past, which gave it the looks of an antique shop more than that of a traditional Irish pub. That evening James arrived first, knowing that his boss would be there in ten minutes, like clockwork. He sat at the counter in the very wooden stool where the editor in chief used to sit, the one right in front of the taps with a black leather covered top, and ordered a pint of Guinness. When the editor arrived, he hollowed the pub owner, then he went to sit down and spotted his reporter at the bar.

"Good evening boss, are you a regular here, too?" said James, his voice still a little shaky.
"As a matter of fact yes, I've been a regular at this pub for forty years now. I've never seen you here, though," replied the man, annoyed.

"I usually come at lunch-break," answered James solemnly, while the pub owner looked at him in astonishment, sure he had never seen him before. "Can I get you a Guinness?"

"If you insist. It is my favourite, after all. Since we're here, how was it with the Gov. inspectors?"

"They grilled me four hours straight, although I don't think it was actually about me at all."

"Of course not. What did they ask you?"

"Mainly of the weirdos of the Village. They were interested in details about the library and the books the old man hides underground."

"Have you told them everything they wanted to know?" asked the editor in chief insistently as he drank his pint.
"Everything I know, sure."

"And did they tell you anything?"

"Nothing. They were distant and standoffish the whole time. They asked me why I went there, who sent me and whether things really happened as I described in the article."

"And what did you say?"

"Well, I said that the Editor in chief sent me and that the events in the article were in fact kind of overstated."

"You fool. A journalist never recants what he writes in his piece! Not unless in court, under oath. Damn! You should know these kinds of things. Where did you do your internship?"

"At 'The Clare Champion'. I was the reporter for their local news column, here in Dublin."

"And how did you get from that tabloid to the Irish Times?"

"Because of the journalism competition."

"Because of... a competition. Well... let's just never talk about this ever again. Ok?"

"But why would the Government even bother about my article?"

"It's not about the article, it's about those people. Nobody wants them around and there they are. Every week on page six. The Government would send them away from those lands, but they never seem to have quite enough leverage. Maybe if they caught them trafficking with something illegal… this time they could finally drive them out and destroy that f... that frigging' Village of theirs!"

"I do not think that some ancient books will constitute leverage enough for this."

"And what would you know about it? Maybe the Government will find out that those books are stolen goods. After all, that doesn't fall far off from what you wrote in your article."

"Yes, but we both know that the article was heavily revised by both you and the editor before going to print. And I still don't get what would the books help with driving the people of the Village away…"

"Heavily revised? Who do you think you are? You… you greenhorn. How dare you think I've had anything to do with your third-rate piece?"

"But... But the editor said…"

"I really don't think he'd say any such nonsense. Anyway, it's time you went home, I'm awaiting company."

"But, boss!" James was bewildered by the reaction of his editor in chief, not to mention dissatisfied at his boss' answers, or lack thereof, to his questions. "We are in a public place! You can't kick me out just like that!"
"Nobody is kicking you out. I'm cordially inviting you to leave, greenhorn. Get lost now, I've got business to attend to."

James was speechless; he stood up but, not in the least intentioned in leaving the premises, he opted for hiding in the adjoining room. He sat on a red-and-brown striped sofa. In front of him was a narrow, high, rectangular table, with a small red stool stored underneath. He was not alone. The place was filling up with all sorts of people getting seated in the various rooms. Within minutes every room in the place was full, even those in the higher floors. From the striped sofa, James tried to keep his boss in sight. He only barely sipped at his beer but he wasn't used to that kind of beverage and soon his bladder started sending alarming messages of weakness, forcing James to ask, with discretion but also with undeniable urgency, the directions to the gentleman's toilets. Upon his return to his solitary seat, he found himself surrounded by unwanted company. He barely had the time to take a look around when one of the boys invited him to sit down in his spot on the sofa. He elegantly declined, hinting at some non-existing company and another seat waiting for him, but the man stood up – he was almost two times James' size – and forced him to sit on the small sofa in the space between himself and his buddy, space made even tighter by the two oversized, sketchy comrades.

"You haven't finished your beer. Heck! You sure you're Irish? We saw you leave the glass half full an' we thought 'here's the little guy, acting all macho and not finishing his ridiculous pint'. We hadn't realized you were going to the toilet," the young giant scolded James, landing a loud slap on his back while the whole party burst into laughs and cheers. Raising his oversized jug he toasted with his friends to the weird and amusing new acquaintance.

"Brewmaster! My friend is done with water, bring him a pint of real beer now!" shouted the mountain to a passing waiter, who swiftly brought in a pint of eight degree Smithwick's.

"For me? No thanks…" James tried to decline, as he felt like he'd already had enough.

"I insist. Another toast to our new friend!" the Viking shouted again, landing another smack on James's back while forcing him to swallow an excellent ruby red drink with the faintest caramel taste.

From the counter, the editor in chief and his two drinking companions kept their eyes on the scene, raising their mugs in the air and toasting to the young reporter's health. Shortly thereafter the man went to James' rescue: "Come with us for a bite to eat, lad. Come on Teddy Bear, let the young one go."

"Boss! Do you know this guy?" answered the huge man energetically, as he drained his fifth giant pint.
"Yes, yes. I know him. Come on James, let's go put some food into your system."

James, half drunk already, waved a tipsy goodbye to his new buddies, took one last pat on the back in response, then was helped up. Staggering, he followed his boss upstairs to a richly decorated room, which embodied in every particular the costumes and tradition of that ancient place, that corner in the deepest part of Ireland.

"Hi, James. My name is Arthur and this is my friend Thomas."

"Hi-ch!" replied James, still experiencing some alcohol-related difficulties. Right then, the waiter entered the room. He was a young man with short almost shaved hair, big brown eyes, and a confident air. Sure he didn't look like some student cashing in on a part-time job at the pub. He rather had the air of a young cadet of some military academy.

"Good evening. What may I bring you?"

"My friends and I will have chicken thighs with sauce."

"And for you the usual, sir?" he looked at James as if hoping his stare could turn the reporter to ashes.
James, half-drunk, couldn't manage to utter a word. Pinned by the waiter's poisonous gaze, nothing else seemed to come out his mouth but:
"Ushal? What is Ushal?"

"James, how on earth can you be drunk on two pints, lad? Yes, just bring him the usual," replied the editor in chief to the waiter dismissively.

"Where did this one leave his manners..." sneered one of his friends, annoyed by the waiter's behaviour.

In the fifteen-minutes wait for their food the three men exchanged some pleasantries with a drunker and drunker James, then the waiter came with their order. A huge platter with a wide range of sausages and other kinds of fried and grilled meat, french-potatoes, and fried onions was set in front of a disconsolate James.

"James, that is a hell of a platter. Do you get to swallow all this stuff at noon and still go back to work? Well, to being young and strong!" commented the editor in chief drinking with his friends, admiring the lad's apparent intestinal prowess. The young journalist couldn't but weakly nod and smile. Finally, he shrugged and started nibbling on a potato.

"He usually scolds me for, he says, the plate is too small," sneered the waiter, staring at James with a serious and sullen expression.

"Bring another pint of beer to the lad. This time maybe a light blonde… Do you still have bottled Peroni?" the editor in chief couldn't wait for the waiter to leave the room.

"He really doesn't like James! Almost as if it were personal. How unprofessional… I'm considering summoning the head waiter and have him give the young man a hard time about his behaviour."

"Forget it. Just look at the lad instead. One or two more mugs tops and he's down for the count."

The evening went on. The three men had many things to talk about, situations to settle, projects to discuss. After another pint, James fell into a deep sleep hugging his plate, his face between what was left of the fried onions and sausages. The editor in chief and his friends left the pub around one o'clock, paying their bill as well as James's and leaving some money for a taxi to get the lad home.

Later that night, after closing up, the pub manager scolded the young waiter.
"Was all that fuss even necessary? Do you know who those people are? You fool! What were you thinking?"

"He started it! First of all, what was he even doing here? We waited for those three to come from York for weeks, and here he comes, the moron, almost ruining everything. And he's a liar!"

"Oh, forget it! Why do I even try to make you see reason? Everything doesn't just always run smoothly as one would like, you know? It happens all the time, plans always get disrupted."

"Then I should be ecstatic that this random stoner, who can't even hold his beers, interferes with our plan preventing us from doing our job?"

"You don't know that he did." answered the blue-eyed man, advancing from the shadows.

"And where did you come from, Hubert?"

"The front door was open. Where is he?"

"But... but I locked that door myself!" replied the pub manager. "Oh, whatever. The journalist is in the v.i.p. room upstairs. He's asleep, perched on his lot."

"You, young boy, you must learn to keep your mouth shut and adjust your behaviour to the unexpected. The old man is right: you were about to blow up our cover, Mark," the blue-eyed man turned to look at the waiter, pointing his finger at him, while with his other hand he played with a bunch of weird keys. They were passepartout.

"I didn't mean to… I lost my temper."

"Forget it, tomorrow you're coming back to the Village, anyway. Give me a hand with the drunkard, will you? I have to bring him home."

"But… To the Village? But we had to…"

"Did you hear what I said? Change of plans, you aren't needed here anymore. Tomorrow you are going back, period."

"Actually, Hubert, the kid has been a great help around here. He's got a good pair of arms, you know? Worked like two waiters."

"You too. Just do as I say and keep your eyes and ears open. Certain events were set in motion and we need to be even more careful now."

****

The next morning the High Priest of the Elm woke up at dawn, got dressed, ate a frugal breakfast, prepared a backpack and took the path across the Village towards the Sacred Wood, where he intended to find Breton and Arkon, ask them for a hawk-a-mole to bring back to the Herbarium and save the day.

"Something's off," he mused. "I've got a thought stuck in my head since yesterday. I feel like I was supposed to do something… but I just can't figure out what. Oh, well. It must have been something irrelevant… Though maybe I keep thinking about it because it was very important. If only I could remember what it was…"

He'd barely entered the thicket, when a voice shouting his name echoed through the trees of the Haunted Forest, shortly followed by Lyon's figure appearing from the bushes.
"High Priest, thank the Goddess I found you. The Government inspectors are here. They insisted on searching the library and are pulling it apart!"

"That's what was eluding me. Hubert called to warn me about them. Quick Lyon, we must return to the Village. I hope those lawyers are still around…"

Upon their entering the library, even before any introduction could take place, the chief inspector exclaimed:

"Here is the old man. And where were you?"

"Good morning officer. I was taking a walk in the woods."

"A walk you say? Yes, yes. Of course. Stop wasting my time, I've been here as long as I can bear already."

"May I be excused? I have to make a couple of phone calls," interjected Lyon trying to get to the landline phone on the desk in the far corner of the room.

"Absolutely not. Stay where you are. Phone calls? Who do you think you are dealing with? We aren't fools or tourists, we won't be distracted by your tricks and tales!"

The High Priest was speechless. He did not understand why that stranger would talk so angrily, with such an arrogant and malicious tone.

"Let's get going, folks. I've got a lot on my plate today. Just take me to the library." said the inspector, grabbing the old man by the arm and jerking him towards the next room.

"Lyon, while I escort our welcome guest to the library, would you please call..."

"He's not doing any such thing. He will come with us, so I can keep an eye on him. You, come here. Now!" he shouted, ordering his men to handle the boy.

"Stop!"

"And who would the old bat be?" asked the inspector acidly, watching the High Priestess advance towards him, accompanied by four men and three women. Thinking they meant to attack him, the officer threatened to have them all arrested.

"I think there's a misunderstanding, sir. It is not our habit to attack people. I only meant to ask, since this is private property, that you show me the mandate that allows you to search the Village's library," answered the woman calm and wisely.

The inspector released violently the High Priest, promptly rescued by the villagers, and headed impetuously towards the elderly priestess.

"Do you think I'm a fool? Do you think I don't know the rules? I represent the Law!"

"All right. Show me your warrant, then."

"I do not need any warrant to inspect a public place!" shouted the officer very close to the woman's face.

"Excuse me if I'm interrupting, but this whole area is on private lands: these streets, buildings, and fields do not even appear on Government's maps, because we are a private facility. You represent the Law, you should know that," intervened a younger priestess.

"What a load of crap!" replied the inspector. In his haste to settle his mission, he had decided to go in without a search warrant, convinced that the people of the Village, uneducated simpletons that they were, wouldn't even know the difference.

"If you don't have one we will still allow you to inspect our library, provided you do it quietly, without making a fuss or threaten anyone. In fact, I can see your colleagues already at work over there," said the High Priestess, knowing that at least four more officers were already searching every corner of the library.

The inspector, annoyed, went back to the High Priest and took him by the arm again, but this time the old man replied calmly:
"I do not need any support, you know? I have two legs for that and, despite my old age, they still work very well."
The inspector silently released his grip and entered the library. Without wasting any more time, he immediately entered the elevator and descended with the High Priest to the chamber where the collection of rare and ancient manuscripts was stored. Meanwhile, John, a friend of Lyon, was desperately trying to get a hold of the two lawyers whom Hubert had advised the High Priest to call days before. Unfortunately, they both were in court, one in Belfast and the other in Dublin. So the young man phoned Hubert, who cussed against how distracted the High Priest was before making another round of calls. Soon a lawyer arrived. He had just opened his personal studio in Donegal and he was very young and inexperienced, but also the only one available so last minute.

"And you say this Code has a regular receipt?"

"Of course inspector, here it is."

"One hundred and seventy thousand pounds? Where did you find all this money? "

"Actually, see, that is the commercial value of the Code. I paid it a lot less. You can see the figure down there."

"Sixteen-thousand pounds? How is it possible?"

"Well… the man needed the money… he did not know whom else to sell this family heirloom to… let's say we came to an advantageous accord. Though I have to admit I wouldn't have paid over fifty-thousand pounds for this, anyway."

"You are telling me, this old pile of battered and badly preserved paper, bound in that filthy leather cover of who knows what kind of creature… you are telling me it's actually worth all that money?"

"Certainly not."

"Well, it seemed…"

"It's actually worth a lot more."

"That… thing? Over a hundred and seventy thousand pounds? I cannot believe it. In any case, these objects should not be hidden in this library of yours, they should be kept in the National Archives in Dublin!"

"I'm sorry to contradict you officer, but these books were regularly purchased therefore they cannot leave this place."

"And who is this one?" asked the inspector addressing the High Priest. The old man was unaware of whom the lad may be, having never seen his face before, but found himself quite fond of him already.

"Allow me to introduce myself. Arthur McFarrey. I'm a lawyer, here are my credentials. As I said, the High Priest can provide all the required paperwork for these books, therefore they will remain exactly where they are," said the lawyer in one breath, red from the emotion of standing up to a Government officer and from holding his breath too long. A drop of sweat slid down his forehead onto his round face while, with some difficulty given his large size, he walked through the narrow door into the collection's chamber.

After a few hours of animated and calm, cheerful and irritating, impetuous and sensible, and even more, useless discussions, the inspection ended. The officers left the library empty-handed, their boss furious like a captive wild beast for failing to take away with him those precious relics and, above all, for not finding the smallest proof of an online sale scam of sorts concerning the reproductions of the manuscripts. Everything was in order. All the books had their paperwork attached, all the documentation certified the High Priest's ownership of each and every one of them and, on the net, they were made available for reasonable figures to whomever wished to have a copy of those precious relics. All the information was advertised in the website as well: within the expedition came a certificate that the volume was a copy conforming to the original and hand-made in the Village laboratory, with even its own progressive number printed on the back. The prices were reasonable, sometimes embarrassing for the hours of work put into the manuscripts' replicas.

As soon as the inspectors left, the High Priest of the Elm resumed his journey to the Haunted Forest. After a long discussion with Breton, who wouldn't even think of lending one of his precious hawk-a-moles to anyone in the Village, the High Priest decided to ask the more malleable Arkon and finally obtaining one, returned to the Village and ran to the Herbarium.

Without waiting for Isabella and her consent, he instructed the creature upon its mission and freed it in the greenhouse.

"High Priest, have you found the hawk-a-mole?" as soon as she saw him wandering around her precious plants, the curator advanced swiftly towards the old man who'd breached her sanitary protocol once again on the same day.

"Yes," replied the High Priest looking up.

"Did you convince Breton?"

"Yup. No, actually, not Breton. It was Arkon. Arkon lent it to me."

"Good. And where is it? Before setting it free I want to make sure it's in good health and above all that it doesn't have more strange magical gibberish that may damage my seedlings."

"Yes, yes." kept answering the old man, completely absorbed in his observation of the creature and almost unaware of Isabella talking to him.

"Don't you tell me… he's already set it free."

"Yup. Oh yes. Yes, yes," replied, finally, the old man, when he could no longer see the creature.

"What have you done?" screamed Isabella, furious.

End of Episode 01

Episode 02
The CONVIVIUM

James woke up with a strong headache. The sunlight filtered through the window bothering him as if he wasn't already in a very sour mood. The nauseating smell of his vomit made his gag reflex weak. He couldn't get to his feet, but he absolutely needed to reach the bathroom. He felt throbbing cramps in the lower abdomen, his bladder ready to explode. The noise of the cars in the street was deafening and pierced incessantly through his head as a sharp, pointy blade, making him want to slide to the ground, stuff his fingers in his ears and scream as loud as he could to muffle their sound. Another gag prevented him from escaping that horrible torture. He couldn't reach the toilet in time, the deafening car horns resonated in his eardrums, migraine seemed to pulsate with his heartbeat increasing the pressure in his head to the verge of explosion. This brought on a new contraction of the stomach, which caused the surge of rancid saliva and acidic gastric fluids. Then, a series of embarrassing intestinal discharges brought James to tears not so much out of pain as of modesty. Even though he was alone, he was ashamed of himself and of how much he'd drunk. The lack of control over his body and his fuzzy memories embarrassed and annoyed him. The pub, the editor in chief, his friends, the big guy, that young obnoxious waiter and then… the blackout. He was on his knees now, his hands grasping for safety on the edge of the bed, the carpet soaked of all the liquids that kept coming out of his body: vomit, liquid faeces and that cold sweat he was drenched in from head to toes.

The smell, a mixture of the fumes of all the waste coming out of his body, was unbearable. So much so, it disgusted James so much it provoked more abdominal contractions. A vicious circle from which there seemed to be no getting out. He had to get to the bathroom as soon as possible, but he didn't know how to do that without spreading the faeces around the apartment. He tried for a slow crawl, but some leakage was inevitable. He hit his fists on the floor in a burst of frustrated rage. In the end, exhausted to the end of his tether, he dragged himself to the bathroom, careless at last of his disgusting trail. Too tired to make any real effort, he stripped naked and curled up on the floor of the shower, stretching his hand out to the faucet to turn on the water. Then the ranting begun, sparked by the iciness of the water that poured on him. James turned the shower off and on repeatedly, cursing. Eventually, he decided to just let the water run, but after a while, it became so scalding hot that he had to turn it off again. In a fit of fury, he violently pounded his fists against the shower's tiles, hurting his hands and then complaining of the self-induced pain. He turned the water back on, screamed, turned it off, knocked his fists on the shower's floor splashing water all around the bathroom, then finally he turned the faucet to halfway. Only then did he find some peace of mind: the water drizzled warm, neither too hot nor too cold. But that peace was ephemeral. In just a handful of seconds, he moved the mixer slightly to the left again, to make the water a little warmer. Of course, it came out scolding hot. To the right, then. Icy cold. Again to the left. Damn it – scolding hot.

***

The following morning at dawn the High Priest of the Elm went to the Herbarium, anxious to make sure that Arkon's hawk-a-mole had fulfilled his duty of finding and disciplining the mysterious creature responsible for the destruction of the Herbarium's plants. As usual, he walked down the gravel path skirting harmoniously the beds of alternate crops and entered the building from the back door. Isabella, the curator, wouldn't even look at him. She was in a flowerbed, talking animatedly with a young girl. When the girl saw the old man, though, she ran to greet him.

"Ildegard! You're so energetic. What are you doing here?"

The young girl crashed into the High Priest of the Elm and hugged him. "I came to help Mrs. Garcia."

"Oh, I see. And what are you helping her with?" He asked smiling and looking into her eyes with a fatherly look.

"We are sowing basil and valerian," she answered in an openly great mood.

"Good morning, Isabella," tried then the old man.

"Mornin'," replied her politely, though never steering her eyes from her occupation.

"By the way, you know she's still angry at you for the havoc your pet caused to our plants…" whispered Ildegard not so inconspicuously in her old friend's ear.

"You think so? It'll pass. Just wait and see," replied the High Priest softly. Isabella looked up, her eyes narrow and beaming towards him, making it clear that the wait would be longer still.

"Any news about the hawk-a-mole? Did you see it at all?"
Isabella gestured with her head towards the beds where the plants from the Sacred Forest were grown. The High Priest of the Elm waved a goodbye to the girl and went to look for the beast in that direction.

"Ilde, come on! We don't want to spend the whole morning planting one basil, do we?" Isabella called to Ildegard in a sweeter voice. She had a soft spot for that girl, whom she saw as a younger herself. Ildegard was more mature than her age and Isabella got along with her quite well. Much better than she did with the old Priest, for sure.

"Will you ever forgive him?" asked the girl naively.
"Of course I will. Eventually. But he must learn that rules are there to be respected. The Herbarium is a delicate place and that's why we must be sure everyone is on their best behaviour in here, always suited up and careful of the plants."

When the High Priest reached the oak in the centre of the lot he peered through the branches to see if there were some traces of the hawk, but he couldn't find any. Then he searched the roots to see if there were anything hidden underneath, still, nothing came out.

It had been almost two hours since the water in the shower had started flowing. James sat there on the damp floor, knees to his chest, hands on his head, an unstoppable swarm of thoughts buzzing in his head. From time to time he'd stretch out his hand to try and make the water warmer or colder. The water concealed any other noise, including the entrance door opening and the footsteps of the housekeeper in the apartment. She came for a couple of hours every two weeks to clean the place, always empty and not quite dirty. Her screams, though, James couldn't help but hear. The woman's squawks took him, and any other person in the apartment building, by surprise. James didn't understand who she might be at first. He grabbed a towel, wrapped it tightly around his waist, turned off the shower and rushed out of the bathroom to see who'd entered his home. Doing so he almost slipped on the trail of vomit and other liquids he'd left on the floor. Meanwhile, by the entrance at the end of the short corridor, a small, stocky, red-haired Portuguese woman was insulting him in her mother tongue. James tried to utter an apologetic answer, but it seemed to just make things worse, as the little lady started throwing plates in his direction, scattering thousands of potentially hurtful ceramic shreds on the floor. Still mumbling to herself the woman took her bag and left the apartment forever, leaving the front door wide open so that James could hear her insults as she descended the stairwell. The noise and the smell drew the attention of the gossipy neighbours, who didn't lose the chance – much to their own detriment – to stick their noses out theirs and into James's apartment. His headache was getting worse every minute. James ran awkwardly towards the entrance, slipped on a pool of his own vomit and fell awkwardly, losing the towel he had tied around his waist to cover himself. The old widows of the building turned away faking disgust, then turned back to take another peak and then just one more through the front door. Some of them even lingered either because, given the old age, they couldn't see very well anymore and weren't sure of what they'd been peeking at, or because they had seen too well what was going on in there and didn't want to miss out on the show that the plump young man, still topsy-turvy and with his member exposed and dangling, was unintentionally making of himself. They wouldn't even care about the stench coming out of the lad's apartment: they didn't see certain things that often anymore, every occasion had to count. Increasingly embarrassed, the boy stood up awkwardly, showcasing his clumsiness even further. He didn't even tie back the towel. Everybody had taken a good look at everything anyway, why bother? There was nothing else to hide, by now. James reached the entrance, half running half limping and all the time hearing the old women screaming out of modesty and squealing out in excitement. Not one of them, though, turned away or went back to their house. Finally, James slammed the door shut. Once the curious widows were locked out of his sight, he sighed, leaning with his back against the door, just in time to hear the whispering in the hallway begin. Little did it matter. He never gave a damn about what they thought. In that precise moment, he set his eyes on the kitchen table, where a large yellow sheet about the size of an A4, with a note on top written in black ink, caught his attention. It wasn't in his writing. He didn't have that kind of paper. He approached the table, picked up the note and started reading.

"Hey Superman, as soon as you wake up I suggest you eat a couple of crackers and honey. Lunch on an apple and a simple unseasoned salad. Drink a lot of water and rest. Your mysterious blue-eyed friend.
By the way, did I mention that I am keeping an eye on you?"

James threw himself on a chair and sighed. Once again that man had entered his house, once again there was no sign of forced entry. Still suffering from the hangover, James called in the police to report the crime.

***

The morning went by quickly at the Herbarium, and it was about lunchtime when a cheeky young man approached the lots. Recognizing her from a distance, the boy called out to his sister:

104

"Ildegard, Ildegard!"

"Stop! You, monster!" shouted back the sweet looking girl, leaving both Isabella and her own brother speechless.

"I must defend the seedlings," she then whispered softly in Isabella's ear. "He'll hurt them."

"Ilde, go easier on your brother. Hi Ryan, your sister is here and, of course, she was joking," replied Isabella to the boy, with a huge smile.

"Good morning Mrs. Isabella, thank you. Ildegard, mom sent me to pick you up. We have to go home," said the boy walking towards them.

"Ryan, you know that if you want to enter the Herbarium you have to wear the proper boots, right?" his little sister scolded him.

The kid took a step back, out of the cultivated lot. "Yes, of course I do. But I'm not entering now. You coming, Ildegard?"

"Ryan! Ryan, come here lad!" the High Priest shouted for the boy as loud as he could manage: after scouring the whole Herbarium he was now in the furthest corner of the magical herbs section, where he'd finally found the hawk-a-mole he was looking for. He seemed, however, unable to catch it alone and was calling out for reinforcements. He didn't have to call him twice: the boy left his sister and the curator behind and run to his mentor. Isabella – definitely losing her temper again – started mumbling in a menacing tone, while martially heading straight towards the two.

"You! You are the worst, most foolish, most reckless… Uneducated of boys. What is it that you have for your brains, dirt? We abide by a few, and I might add very simple, basic rules here. How comes you two of all people never manage to follow even one of them? Where do you think you are? High Priest you, you are a lost cause, and even though, I still can hardly stand you. But you, Ryan. What did I always, what has your sister just told you?"

"Well…"

"No. Not well. Where – are – your – boots."

"Come on, Isabella, it was I who called for him…"

"Silence. I'm really disappointed."

"But…"

"It seems to me that there's some scolding going on here. Can't you even tell when it's time to shut the trap?"

"… too late. It's gone."

"What? What's gone? I'll tell you. My patience's gone. Oh but I'm in charge now, you'll see."

"Isabella, what with all the screaming? What have they done now?" interjected the High Priestess of the Elm, just arrived at the Herbarium for her weekly shift.

"These two scoundrels here, think they are above all rules. They enter and leave without ever following the protocol."

"Is that true?" asked the woman to the boy and her husband. Their eyes glued to the ground and speechless, the two knew that the curator had all the reasons in the world to be mad at them.

"Have you got nothing to say?" said the High Priestess, while Isabella looked superciliously at them, her arms crossed as her mood.

"Very well, then. Guess who's going to take care of table service and dishwashing for the whole week next week. Starting tomorrow. We'll see if, next time you set foot in here, you manage to follow some simple clothing rules."

"That's it?" asked Isabella, wishing for a more punitive penalty.

"Isabella, I believe this will be all. You will see, give them one solid week of chores and these two will show you how they have learned their lesson. And now, out of here. Both of you."

"But…"

"What now?"

"I was here to work on your problem. I found the hawk-a-mole and I really – really – needed the boy to lend me a hand to flush it out. I wanted to see if he'd found our mysterious parasite, already. That's why I called out to Ryan. But with all these screams, now the hawk-a-mole is long gone. I'll have to start looking for it from the top. Don't you want to find out what's been destroying your plants?" asked the High Priest to the curator. Isabella just turned away from him and didn't say a word.

"This doesn't give you the right to break the rules of Isabella's Herbarium," replied the High Priestess of the Elm.

Meanwhile, Ryan and Ildegard had run back to their home. On the way there, they crossed Eleonor's path, and upon seeing her the girl shouted:
"Ryan was punished! Ryan was punished!"

Eleonor stopped her: "What did he do?" asked her, incredulous. That boy never did anything wrong.

"I have no idea. But Isabella was furious, and then the High Priestess of the Elm said that Ryan and the High Priest will do the dishes for the whole week!"

"What? The High Priest got punished, too?" Eleonor went from astonished to stunned. Never she'd have thought anyone could do something as inconceivable as punishing the old wise man.

"You don't want to end up like them, do you?" Eleonor rebuked the kid for her insolence towards her brother and the High Priest. Ildegard instantly shut up, her face red like a tomato. She waved Eleonor goodbye and ran home to tell the news to her mother. Eleonor turned back and went to look for Lyon. She meant to reach him as soon as possible, to report to him the unusual news.

***

It so happened that the two policemen who responded to James' call were the same ones that had taken his previous one. As soon as they entered the apartment they exchanged a disgusted look. The stench made the air unbreathable. James, still agitated and wearing nothing but a pair of jeans, tried to show them that the same guy had broken into his apartment again.

"Have you been drinking this time, too?" Asked the tall one, sneering from under his moustache. James didn't answer the question. Instead, he asked the two policemen to do something already, cause he couldn't stand even the idea of a stranger coming and going from his house whenever he felt like, anymore.

"Did they steal something this time?"

"Not that I know of, no. I don't... I don't think so."

"Would you care to explain for us, whom exactly you think we should look for, why should we look for them and also where are we supposed to look for them? And just one more thing: did you host a frat party in your house? Alcohol, drugs, sex... The smell is so bad you can't breathe in here."

"No! Is just... last night at the pub..."

"You had a little too much to drink, is that so?"

"Well... I think so."
"And at the end, someone drove you back home. They did you a favour, you know?"

"I... cannot remember."

"You're just wasting our time!" exclaimed the other policeman, signalling not so subtly to his colleague that James was probably a closeted homosexual who'd partied too much.

"So, last night. You drink beer after beer until you get wasted, then your 'friend' is so nice to bring you home… and you can't remember a thing after that," the tall cop made a recap, smiling mischievously and winking at James to stress the double entendre.

"Did he hurt you?" Continued the other, unconsciously moving his hands to his back pockets.

"No… But, wait. What are you implying?"

"Oh, come on Mr. O'Dael. It's clear from the note you showed us that you have a fervent admirer. He calls you 'Superman', describes himself as 'your blue-eyed friend', protects you… A certain somethin' must have happened here yesterday night. Maybe with a little help from your friend, some coke or one of those nice blue pills… It's the only scenario that can explain why you would be so completely dazed this morning. That and hormones. Except you don't remember a thing. You will see, tomorrow your memories will start to float back, and then you'll call your friend for a laugh and another night of whatever it is that two boys do when lights go down."

"No. What? No! None of that… What are you implying…?"

"Kid, you told us you can't remember a thing. And even if you did, as we told you the other time, we cannot help you. Unless the reason for this call was that you like men in uniform. If that be the case, we really must ask you to stop calling or we'll report you to the station. I am sure you will have better luck in one of the clubs downtown, anyways. Plenty of drags and trannies will love to share a fantasy or two with that juicy ass of yours…"

"Anyhow, you better stop with the calls and all. Next time we will report you for harassment. Just call a good shrink – a woman, possibly – and stop wasting our time."

In the midst of this verbal exchange, James' girlfriend was coming up the stairs. She was a girl in her twenties, a university student with large, round, thick glasses, long, thin hair, a graceful, delicate and slightly elongated face and prominent ears. And of course, she'd heard every single word: the shock still lingering in her gaping pupils was quite evident. The two policemen left the apartment, taking their hats off to salute the petrified girl on the staircase.

"That's what it is? You, having the time of your life in gay nightclubs?" She started screaming without even saying hello or crossing the threshold, the veins in her neck swollen and throbbing to the rhythm of her suddenly onset fury.

"But…"

"Partying with fags! You disgust me. You piece of shit. Pervert! You know what? Fuck you! I am breaking up with you. Now go sobbing to your little friends. See if anyone consoles you," the girl grabbed James' keys from her purse, threw them at him and ran off crying down the stairs to her car. She got on the minivan and drove away. The old spinsters and widows of the building, who had been listening and watching the scene from their peepholes, cheered the girl with silent applause.

The two policemen, upon their arrival at the station, filled in a heavy report on James O'Deal, labelling him as an alcoholic and a pervert.

Alone, at last, James shut the door and barricaded himself at home, which seemed the only thing left to do, given the turn that that damn day had taken. He cleaned the apartment thoroughly while thinking about his next move. The world, his world, had crumbled and he couldn't seem to find a solution to the devastating turn his life had taken.

***

After supper, Ryan and the High Priest of the Elm met in the kitchen and found themselves in front of a mountain of dishes, bowls, glasses and cutlery that needed washing. The old man shook his head in resignation.

"I'm sorry you got involved in this, Ryan. Believe me, it was not my intention."

"No problem, High Priest. Besides, you know I'd follow you to the end of the world, what's washing a few dishes?"

The two went on with their chore. Ryan scrubbed and rinsed the dishes, while the High Priest dried them and placed them in the cupboard. The old man's thoughts were on the Herbarium. He must track down the hawk-a-mole and he still didn't know how. He was silent when he wasn't answering to Ryan's incessant questions, the only thing that would interrupt his musings.

When they finished with the dishes, they went to the Herbarium bringing small electric torches for lighting. They immediately went to the lot of the Sacred Forest plants to resume their research.

Looking out of her bedroom's window, Eleonor noticed two lights zigzagging into the Herbarium:
"I wonder… maybe this time we'll catch who's been destroying the plants…?" the girl muttered to herself under her breath. She didn't know that those lights were the torches of Ryan and the High Priest. She grabbed a jacket and she was out, headed to her boyfriend Lyon's house.

"Found nothing yet?" shouted the High Priest under his breath.

"Nothing. It's not here."

"We've looked everywhere in this lot, let's go over to the spices."

Lyon, Eleonor, Mark, and Melissa arrived at the Herbarium meaning to seize the culprits of the devastation of Isabella's plants.

"For the Goddess, who's there? What are those lights?" exclaimed the High Priestess of the Elm, looking out of her dining room's window, over to the Herbarium. Without wasting a moment she threw on a robe and went out, keen on catching the culprits of the Herbarium's disarray, once and for all. She went straight to Isabella's who, baffled and irritated, collected all the villagers she could find in the streets and rushed with the mob to her personal Sancta Sanctorum.

"I wonder where my husband is?" asked the High Priestess of the Elm, as she recalled not having seen him home after dinner at all.

"He'll be in the library, as always," answered Isabella in a dismissive tone.

"That would be odd, though. By this time he's usually in bed snoring like an old bear during wintertime…" replied the High Priestess of the Elm, a touch of concern in her voice.

"Nothing. Not even the hint of nothing. But I know it must be around here."

"Don't worry. We will find it, you'll see," replied Ryan, remembering that he hadn't told her mother he'd be out late with the High Priest and hoping she wouldn't worry too much.

"What's going on out here? Has anyone seen my son?" asked Brigitte worriedly. She was out looking for her son, Ryan, who'd not come home after dinner. She had been first to Lyon's house and hadn't found there his son nor the other kid, so she'd thought she'd go to the library, maybe she'd find her son there with the High Priest of the Elm. On the way, she had met the villagers whom Isabella was guiding to the Herbarium.

"Brigitta, what are you doing out so late?" asked a priest.

"I'm looking for my son. I'm beginning to worry, you don't happen to know where he is, do you?"

"Did you try at Betty's?"

"No. I don't think he'd be at hers. I went to look for him at Lyon's, but I couldn't find him there, either of them."

"They'll be somewhere together, planning some prank or training. You know how Lyon is a father figure to Ryan."

"Yes, but this late at night? And Lyon's parents told me that Eleonor came to their house a while ago and that they both left with Marc and Melissa. He's too young to be out with them at night."

"There! Found it! Ryan, move it! Point the light here!"

"I'm here, I'm here! Where is it? Where do you want the light?"

"Here! Point it under the branches of this rosemary!"

"I'm ready, here I come!"

"Careful! It may attack you and I can assure you it's small and cute and all, but its bite hurts a great deal."

"I'll try, anyway… Ouch! It bit me! Ouch!"

"Ryan! Let me see. What did I tell you? It almost bit your finger off your hand. Come. I have a handkerchief, if we wrap it around the cut it will slow the blood flow."

"There it is! Here, wait… it's almost… it's… I'm close… there! I caught it!" exclaimed Ryan diving on top of a small animal running around in the dark. At the same time, the High Priest of the Elm was closing his net on the elusive hawk-a-mole he'd managed to corner against the rosemary plant, blinded and disoriented as it was by the light of the torches.

"What are you talking about, Ryan? I've got the hawk-a-mole here, in my hands."

"I don't know what this is, but… it's so cute. It's licking my wound!"

"Let me see," said the old man, turning to shine the light of the torch on the creature that was licking Ryan's hands.

"Look at that. Of all the creatures of the Sacred Forest, I should have known it would be you. It's a dormogoof. That's why the hawk-a-mole wasn't doing its job: these two are great friends. The dormogoof procures for the hawk-a-mole the small ground worms it cannot dig out of the ground on its own. Ground worms are a real delicacy to the hawk-a-mole."

"What are these voices?" wondered Melissa aloud as the group slowly approached the place where they saw the torchlights moving around. They heard more voices coming from somewhere behind them.

"I thought I heard Ryan's voice!" said Brigitta upon entering the Herbarium with the High Priestess of the Elm, Isabella and their party of villagers.

"I think I heard it, too. It came from the Herbarium… What is he doing here? Wasn't one punishment enough for one day?" the High Priestess of the Elm was beginning to lose her patience.

Lyon, Eleonor, Melissa and Marc exchanged knowing looks and rushed to the laboratory, where the High Priest of the Elm was placing the two animals in two comfortable though sturdy cages.

"It still looks like a tiny squirrel to me…" was saying Ryan, looking curiously at the tiny rodent-like creature.

"Look better. Observe the grey and brown fur. And if you flip it on the back… here, just like that, see? The fur on the belly is much lighter. And look at the tail, It is always straight up. Squirrels tend to curl it downwards. This is a dormogoof alright. A graceful creature. It distinguishes itself as well from the

121

dormouse of the Glis-glis family for its ears. Its are long and pointy, whilst the dormouse has small and rounded ones. Furthermore, the dormogoof has light brown eyes, rather than black. Look how cute it is. It must have been moved here while he was asleep in the roots of one of the plants Isabella transplanted from the Haunted Forest."

"Ryan! Ryan, are you there?"

The boy stopped mid-motion. He remembered again that he hadn't warned his mother of his plans with the High Priest of the Elm for that night. The old man noticed his agitation and answered in his stead.

"Yes, yes. He is in here with me."

"Good evening, High Priestess."

Marc appeared suddenly from behind a tall bush, intercepting the High Priestess of the Elm and her group.

"And you're here too?" Isabella was becoming suspicious.

"Of course. Didn't the High Priest of the Elm tell you?"

"Tell us what?" snapped the High Priestess of the Elm.

"Em… Well…"

"That tonight we'd be hunting for the creature that is ruining all the plants of the Herbarium!" intervened Melissa, coming out of the bushes behind Marc.

"Melissa, you too?" asked the High Priestess of the Elm in a reassured tone, instantly more relaxed thanks to the presence of her favourite.

"Of course! We have been working hard to help Isabella!"

"No. The High Priest of the Elm didn't warn me at all. Probably because I would have been absolutely against it all, why given the recent happenings," shouted the curator looking straight at the two kids standing in front of her, so suspiciously wearing the statutory boots and gloves without even having been reminded of them by her. At that moment, the deputy curator arrived, puffing and panting and still only half dressed.

"Sorry Isabella, I forgot to tell you. The High Priest told me to tell you, but I never had a chance…"

"Did he now? And when would he have told you? We were together all day today, even at dinner!"

"Were we? No, wait. I mean… Ah, yes! When I went back to the club. We had a coffee," the High Priestess of the Elm scoffed: her husband rarely went to the club, much less offered or drank any coffee. Still, she didn't call out the lie.

"Is this the kind of thing you think it's ok to forget to tell me?"

"Ladies and gentlemen! We finally discovered the culprit of the devastation occurred to Isabella's Herbarium!" the High Priest of the Elm intervened, bringing that embarrassing moment to an end.

"High Priest. I see you are wearing your gloves, boots, apron and mask this time. So it seems you can remember to follow rules if you are motivated to. I do not seem to recall giving my permission to no one, ever, to wander unsupervised in the middle of the night among my precious plants… You haven't injured any of them, have you?"

"Oh, curator Isabella. I didn't see you there. Look, I bring you the culprit: it was a dormogoof."

"A dormo-what?" asked the deputy director incredulously.

"A dormogoof. A small creature very fond of roots and fresh leaves as well as of autumn fruits of the woods, such as acorns, chestnuts, berries, and cranberries. It can sustain itself on some kinds of mushrooms, as well. Still, I honestly don't understand why it went down so hard on the Herbarium plants."

"Good evening everyone! What a wonderful night. And more so, in the magical atmosphere of the Herbarium…"

"Eleonor! Do you know where Ryan is?" asked Brigitta, breaking the astonished silence at the appearance of the young girl, whom everyone favoured for the firmness and determination of character, so uncommon to her young age. Above all and contrary to her friends, she had never shown any inclination to transgressions and rule breaking. If she was there at that time in the night, there must have been a very good reason and no rule breaking involved, which made everyone – even the strict Isabella – instantly feel reassured.

"He's here with me," answered Lyon.

"Hello, mum." chirped the boy giving his most innocent look.

"Eheheh! If you're looking for Ryan, all you need to know is where Lyon is," joked the High Priest of the Elm loud and cheerfully.

"Is the whole entire Village here tonight? No, seriously, is anyone still back at the Village?" asked a priestess in amused amazement, while the High Priestess of the Elm laughed silently imagining – knowing her husband so well – what must have actually happened that evening.

"So, a dormogoof... And why did it take so long for the hawk-a-mole to find it?" asked Isabella only just beginning to realize that the existence of her precious plants was safe at last, as the initial burst of rage had been quenched by the presence of the four kids whom she held in high esteem.

"The hawk-a-mole is a bizarre creature. It's great for patrolling and keeping an eye on things, but it is also incredibly easy to bribe. Especially by the dormogoof, who knows it so well. It's really possible that, as it realized it was being watched by the hawk-a-mole, the dormogoof brought to it some choice food, in exchange for a lifelong harvesting permit in the area under its watch," explained the High Priest of the Elm. Meanwhile, a very worried Brigitta was asking Ryan how he'd got hurt.

"Delicacies? The dormogoof offered my defenceless little plants – roots, rhizomes and all – to the very same thing we asked it to flush out?"

"Not exactly. The hawk-a-mole is more keen on those cute little worms that populate the fertile ground below the crops. I'm talking about those pink- and brownish earthworms."

"Clever dormogoof. But now we must find out why it destroyed all the plants," said the deputy director, who was finally recovering from the run to the Herbarium.

"The most plausible explanation to the dormogoof's devastation is for it to be at least partly involuntary. I will have to study the case more thoroughly tomorrow in my library. Now I'm very tired and I need to rest."

"Ouch! Mom… it hurts!"

"We must clean it and patch it up."

"How did you get hurt?"

"The doormogoof bit his finger in the commotion."

"Go to the infirmary. We need to get that bite checked for infection."

"Why didn't you warn me that you would be here with the High Priest of the Elm and the other kids? Do you have any idea how long I've been looking for you? You should know better, and behave better, too."

"Brigitta, I must step in and apologize. This time it was all my fault. It was supposed to be me and the older kids but, as we had just been washing the

128

dishes together, I asked Ryan to come help us out. I promised him that I would send someone to warn you, but I forgot completely," intervened the High Priest of the Elm winking slyly in the direction of the other kids.

"Tomorrow morning I'll come in to check on all the mess you've made. Right now it's late and we're all tired and cold. Let's just go back to our homes and our beds. Tomorrow we have an early rise."

"Like every morning of every day," added the deputy director in an ironic voice. Eleonor grabbed Ryan by the shoulders and started walking rapidly towards the infirmary.

"As soon as he's all disinfected and patched up I'll take him home myself, Brigitta."

"Thanks, Eleonor. Ryan, I'll wait up for you, don't be late!"

On the way to the infirmary, Eleonor scolded Ryan once again: "You were lucky I realized before them… You, irresponsible… Of course, I can not really yell at you much. The High Priest is the adult,

he's supposed to be the responsible one. But don't even think you're getting away with this!"
"But… Eleonor."

"Shut up and walk fast, before I make you," added Lyon, who was escorting them. "You were punished just today for breaking Isabella's rules, and what do you do? You enter her Herbarium at night, with torches, without warning either your mom, who's in charge of you or the curator, who's in charge of the Herbarium, only to go and break Isabella's rules again! I had to ran to get the deputy out of bed and into the greenhouse to cover your punk ass…"

"And what about the mess we put ourselves in, breaking into the laboratory to get scrubs for all of us and the two of you as well… oh just forget it!" Concluded Eleonor as they entered the infirmary.

"You're right, we didn't stop to think about what we were doing. We just dove in. Thank the Goddess we have at least managed to find the solution to the curator's problem," replied Ryan, dejected for the reprimand, especially as it came from Eleonor and Lyon. He admired them both very much – idolized them, in fact – and he followed them everywhere especially Lyon, who sometimes treated him like a younger brother although sometimes had a hard time getting the younger boy off his back. Ryan was at that age when, at times, one can become a bit intrusive.

During the following days, the High Priest of the Elm studied the two little creatures before at last releasing them both back to the Haunted Forest. Isabella still held a grudge for the casualties that had occurred amongst her plants during that night, but soon even she got past the episode and everything went back to normal. Nonetheless, the High Priestess of the Elm privately scolded her husband, reminding him that she was not stupid and had well understood what really happened that night, and that the only reason she'd decided not to say a word to the curator was to protect Ryan, who had no responsibility for her husband's irresponsible, reckless actions.

The weekend came when the High Priest of the Elm had planned the visit of Mr. Corrige and his wife to the Village. They had called to confirm their arrival for Saturday in the early morning. The High Priest waited for them in the parking lot outside the Village, but lunchtime came and went and they did not appear, nor answered their mobiles.

"Look where you brought me. We're in the middle of nowhere…"
"We're in Ireland, honey."

"I didn't know Ireland for a deserted island!"

"But, my dear, we did see loads of people in the streets on our way here."

"And you wouldn't even properly charge your phone! What if my mother needs to call us about the children? You and your stupid, crazy ideas. You'll do just about anything to make my life a living hell!"

"But, my dove, you told me you would give this a chance…"

"Of course I did! What choice did I have, you've already decided everything!"

"But… but you told me, you had to see the place with your own eyes before…"

"Sure. What did you expect? I'm not saying yes unless I approve. Surely not just to make you happy. I'm feeling bad about it, already. Look where we are. There is nothing but uncultivated land out here. Not even a town in sight, let alone a city…"

"Maybe you haven't noticed, but on our way here we passed dozens of towns and cities…"

"Those straggles of crappy tumble-down houses, that's what you call a city?"

"Actually they were cottages…"

"Yes, yes. Of course. You're always right."

"A very good morning to you!" intervened the High Priest of the Elm.

"And what does this white-haired weirdo wants with us?" whispered the woman to her husband.

"White-haired weirdo? Darling, that's the High Priest of the Elm. I mentioned him to you."

"And he mentioned you to me, as well. Though he forgot to say how elegant and beautiful his wife is, on top of all your other qualities," added the High Priest trying to quench the tension.

"And he's a pimp, too!" whispered again the woman, whilst rapidly making up her mind to run from that hellish hole once and for all, as soon as she got a chance.

"I have been waiting for you. We tried to contact you the whole morning: we thought you might have got lost on your way here. But it doesn't matter now. Come, I will escort you to the banquet myself."

"Is he implying that we're late? Did we come here to be insulted?"

"No, my love. Though you know perfectly well that we had an appointment over three hours ago…"

"And where did he say he's taking us?"

"To lunch, madam. I will personally escort you to the Village's Convivium for our lunchtime banquet. As the usual lunchtime has already passed, I'd beg you to please follow me without further ado. I don't want to make our commensals wait any longer."

"There are others at our table? And they're waiting for us to eat? What kind of place is this? Where did you take me?"

The High Priest of the Elm turned towards Mr. Corridge with a stern gaze. The man shrugged and looked up feigning a sudden admiration of the sky. Without another word, the old man began his walk towards the village.

"Where is he going? Is he leaving us here in the middle of nowhere? Do something! Oh, I want to go home… Don't just stand there like an idiot! You and your stupid ideas. So what, now? Well? Are you going, or what?"

Finally, Mr. Corrige put his hands in his pockets, glanced at his wife, then followed the High Priest of the Elm.
"Mr. Corrige, do not dare challenge me! Come back immediately! I am serious!" she started screaming, offended.

Her husband turned to look at her for a moment, then turned back and continued on his way. Mrs. Corrige, furious, started following the two men in a half run, to keep their hasty pace.

"You're going to pay for this, oh yes. You're going to pay dearly! When we go back home tomorrow, you'll see. You, churl. You…ignorant! Hey, wait for me! I'm in high heels, for Christ' sake! Oh, if you weren't the father of my children… I would have kicked you out long ago!"

Finally, she took off her shoes to manage to keep the men's pace on the dirt path. When she thought she'd come close enough, she threw the shoes against her husband's back. Her act was so clumsy, though, that the man didn't even bother to look back at her. After the outburst, she had to go after her shoes, landed in the grass patches along the path. Then she followed the two men from a distance, unable to reach them without breaking into an uncomfortable and undignified run.
"Hey! How long to the camp? We must have been walking thirty minutes, already. Where the hell did you take me?"

"Actually, the Village is at about five minutes from the parking lot. And you will be able to rest soon. We're almost there," replied the High Priest of the Elm without turning to look at the woman, advancing at his mellow pace helped by a long white walking stick.

"Have you heard? We're almost there," echoed her husband in a higher and quite harsher tone.

"Mr. Corrige, I'm not here to be your shoulder!" replied the old man, slightly annoyed.

"You see? It's always like this. Even this people immediately recognized you for the dumbass you are. Even they know what you're made of," raged the wife, slowly gaining ground.

"Mrs. Corrige you too, please. We're almost there. I wish there weren't any fights, discussions or bickering at my table."
"At last! Welcome to our Village. Did you have a smooth journey?" asked a red-haired girl, Melissa, whom upon their appearance in the distance had been sent forward to greet the welcome guests.

"Melissa. I am sorry for the delay. Everybody's at the table already, I guess."

"Of course, High Priest. We've all been waiting for yourself and your guests!"

"Very well. Be a darling now, go ahead with them and have the lady sit between my wife and the Great High Priestess, and the husband between your father and Hubert. By the way, he's come, right?"

"Of course. He was waiting for you in the library, but then lunchtime came and we rang the bell. So must they be kept very sep…"

"Just do as I told you, Melissa. I will be joining you in a minute," replied the High Priest of the Elm, anticipating the girl's observation which keen as it may be, would have proved uncomfortable at that moment when the matter sure didn't need any further underlining.

"Follow me, please. I will show you where the toilets are, to wash your hands after the long journey," chimed Melissa, without any further comment on the matter.

The old priest left the couple in the young girl's hands. He had to take care of a small business before lunch: his raterpillar needed feeding.

***

Looking out the window of his apartment, he could see the trees of the park nearby the Stefan Karadzha secondary school, his school, on Bratja Bakston. Kristian had recently turned seventeen. Although he was born in Moscow, in his blood run the deepest soul of his Country, Bulgaria. A melting pot of Eurasian ethnic groups overlapping over the centuries. Starting with the proto-Bulgarian tribes, from which his father proudly derived his roots, continuing with the Kazakh invaders, from whom his mother boasted her origins. Thracians, Slavs, Greeks, Romans, Byzantines, Huns, Ottomans, Russians. If one really looked at him, they would find in his features something of each of the ethnic heritages he was a product of. Growing up with traditionalist parents, his interest and knowledge of his roots had grown with him. And while his peers were more and more westernised from the never-ending novelties of the consumeristic western Countries, Kristian studied, researched, discovered the greatness of his People. Through the internet some years back he had discovered the community of the Village, which he now followed and of which some of the younger members were his friends. Even though his English was far from perfect, he somehow managed to understand and be understood. He was a huge fan of the High Priest of the Elm for his work with the Library. Kristian believed that in his collection there must be texts that would help with his research. Moreover, he loved those people. From them, he'd taken inspiration for the project he was developing for his own people. In them he'd recognized the same free spirit of the original populations of his Country, a spirit to which, as soon as he'd have found a way, he meant to give a new voice. This passion sometimes exceeded the limit and often became almost an obsession to him. His younger siblings found him insufferable, his mother did not look favourably at his choices and several times they'd ended up discussing his ideas, his thoughts and his English and Irish friends. His father had threatened to take away his computer and any other "infernal device" that he used to keep in touch with that world. Meanwhile, the young man was preparing and perfecting his plan, as the place where he lived got more and more claustrophobic to him. His desires had become necessities and his passion an obsession to which he had to respond. He stood by the window, scanning the treetops near the horizon with his dark brown eyes. But he didn't see them, his focus was on the list of necessities he'd have to carry on his journey. On his unauthorized journey.

End of Episode 02

Episode 03
FRIENDS

James got some days off. Informed of what had happened to him, the editor in chief couldn't withhold him some days of rest, just enough time to straighten up his thoughts. Truth was, the young journalist knew what he had to do. There were many questions that needed answering, and he thought he had a pretty good idea where to start. First thing first: the pub. The pub owner must answer his questions, there was no denying him the identity of the young waiter who'd been so disrespectful that evening. And he surely must know who the blue-eyed man was. He was a stranger to him, why shouldn't he answer his curiosity? Clueless as to salvage his own love life, he saw in that indecipherable attempt a semblance of pride, which would give him the courage to face that young girl, so upset by what she'd heard from the staircase to his flat. James was at his third beer now. He was trying to straighten up his mind but he wasn't completely lucid, and what seemed simple at first was gradually turning into an impenetrable maze. Right then, a huge slap resounded on his shoulder, whit the tone of a very dull bell. Just the right amount of shock he needed to get out of the daze he'd fallen into.

"James! How ya doin'?" it was one of the editor in chief's friends, a bit rough and not very nice, whom James had had the pleasure to meet that night when his troubles had begun.

"Did you recover from the other night, already?"

"Yup."

"I see. And you are drinking today, too!" continued the other.

"No."

"Oh, come on. Can you only give me one-word sentences? Hey, you, bring out here three pints! And don't bring me the crap this loser is swallowing. I want proper ale!"

"Hey!" James hinted at a reaction.

"Can you hear yourself speak? You are giving me nothing but monosyllables. Now, relax and tell me: did you come back to meet the blue-eyed man?"

"And what would you know on the matter?" asked the young man, as the barman brought three strong dark beers at their table.

"First thing first, where are your manners? When someone asks you a question, it's only proper that you answer before you ask your own question," replied the other, in a serious tone.

"I…"

"Nothing. You keep on with the monosyllables. Your boss speaks well of you, but ours… He'd have already kicked your butt," said the man, crashing his fist on the table.

"You already know the answer, otherwise you wouldn't have asked the question."
"Smart and impertinent. What do you think? Should we forgive him?"

"We have to. The boss said we mustn't twist a hair on his head. If he cooperates and becomes our friend, I see no reason to mess up his haircut," said the younger man, stroking the journalist's hair.

***

The sun set on the Village, leaving the way for the light of the great bonfire that was lit every evening in the centre of the Village. The cracking sounds of the burning wood warmed the souls and hearts of theVillage's inhabitants, who enjoyed the welcoming atmosphere and met once again to tell each other about their day. The days were getting longer in that late spring, though still not warm enough to be called summer. Dinner was almost ready. The Great High Priestess was getting old and preoccupied with her unresolved problems, so she found the dealing with the numerous activities of the country was becoming increasingly difficult. She delegated more and more of it all to her deputy, the High Priestess of the Elm, who actively managed and coordinated the life of the Village assisted by her sisters and her husband, High Priest of the Elm and head librarian – who actually, even though he didn't mean to, ended up creating more problems than he solved. Like what had happened at the Herbarium, for which the curator still harboured resentment against him. Everyone was busy getting ready for dinner and the High Priest of the Elm was setting up the large tables under the tent for the Convivium. It was the place where all the inhabitants of the Village, spontaneously and without any obligation, used to get together for the three most important moments of the day: breakfast, lunch, and dinner. They could cook and eat at home, as well – each house was equipped with a kitchen – so not all the inhabitants of the Village were always present. The Convivium was the most important venue for social gatherings in the Village. While enjoying a good meal, the villagers could discuss their day and their upcoming plans. They laughed at the small incidents that had involved one or another and laid the groundwork for new commissions or odd jobs to improve the life in the Village. Everything was discussed at the Convivium: life in the country and abroad, the news of the world, the children's mischiefs and shenanigans, and the hard work everyone put in fulfilling the tasks they were assigned for the day.

"So, we have glasses, cutlery… let's see if anything's missing," the High Priest of the Elm mused aloud. Then he heard in the distance the unmistakable voice of his dear friend Charlie, and he dropped everything to run meet him. His wife, who was looking at him, rolled her eyes:
"What now? Why are they here already? Why doesn't he ever warns me of anything? We have very welcome guests and he just forgets to let me know. Brigitta, go warn the boys. We'll need to bring over a couple more tables."

"Charlie! Charlie, my dear old friend! What brings you here?" The two men embraced as brothers, and their beards almost ended up tied together in a knot.

"Don't tell me... Did you forget? Don't you remember what day today is?"

"Oh… of course I do?"

"Did you forget about our first meeting?"

"Ah! No. Of course not!"

"You're such an old man!" exclaimed Charlie, sure that the High Priest of the Elm, weak of memory as he was, had indeed forgotten their annual appointment to celebrate their long friendship.

"I even called you, last week, to remind you."

"I did not forget. It's just… I have too many things to do. Sometimes stuff just slips out of my mind!"

"I believe you. A druid like yourself cannot forget certain things," once the High Priest had properly greeted Charlie he went on to greet all his friend's company, while Charlie did the same with the villagers. The first he went to greet, with great joy, was the young Lyon.

"Come here boy, give me a hug! So, when are the two of you getting married?" Eleonor, Lyon's girlfriend, who was not far away, blushed.

"Welcome Charlie, I mentioned that you'd probably arrive today… but you know how he is. He just didn't listen."

"Next time I'm warning you. At least I'll be sure not to find you all unprepared," replied the old friend moving on to hug the young girl as well.

"Will you look at that! Eleonor, you're becoming more beautiful every day!"

"Charlie, you make me blush!"

"It doesn't matter: worst case scenario, you will be even more beautiful with a little red on your cheek. So, when are you locking him up for good?"

"Charlie!" Eleonor's father intervened, embracing his mutual friend and his brothers.

Not far away, hidden in the darkness, a shadow spied the inhabitants of the Village among bushes of oleander and currant, whispering a litany in an unknown and incomprehensible language.

Charlie and his clan came from Duncarron, the ancient fortress they had rebuilt near Edinburgh, in Scotland. They were not Celts however, good Scots that they were, they had joined the cause of the Village and ever since the beginning, the two communities had formed a bond of fraternal friendship. They used to visit each other. In the autumn, a delegation of villagers went to Duncarron. In the spring, on the occasion of the anniversary of their first meeting, Charlie returned the visit to the Village with some members of his clan.

"High Priestess, my congratulations. Every year, I find both you and this Village in even better shape than the year before. I can see all the progress and improvements you are making. This is no longer a Village, now, but a town." the Scotsman complimented the High Priestess of the Elm.

"Charlie, since when have we become formal? Come here and hug me, you old rascal!"

"Hey, hey! Easy with the mushy stuff you two," intervened the High Priest of the Elm, making everyone smile.

148

After the greetings, everybody sat down at the tables. They spent a couple of hours eating, talking, drinking pint after pint of beer and apple cider, and telling each other funny anecdotes and stories of the year past. Then, the time came to play some music. The lights of the torches and the crackling fire were fundamental ingredients to create that warm, comfortable, serene, unparalleled atmosphere. Charlie did not need much encouragement. He lived for this. He stood up from the table, recomposed his thick grey beard, nodded to his companions and as soon as he could embrace his precious bagpipes, he started the dance. The drums echoed in the streets of the Village as their sound waves expanded over the outskirts of the Haunted Forest to the Plane's Grove and the precious plants of the Sacred Wood. A pressing rhythm, punctuated by the imperious sound of the bagpipe and embellished by the groove of an electric guitar. The villagers and their guests didn't wait much to join in. Some gave in to the unrestrained rhythm and threw themselves in the dances, traditional style, others went to pick up their instruments and joined the Scottish group, some of the young girls joined with their sweet voices the swirling and intensely masculine sounds, tormenting the soul of unsuspecting strangers which remained enchanted, with chicken thighs between their teeth or drinking cider from now empty jugs, dazed by that ancient, traditional, ethnic, Scottish and Celtic atmosphere.

***

"What are you plotting?" Kristian's sister asked stiffly, as she caught him still looking at the sky out of the window. He turned his eyes from the foliage of the trees, blew on his bangs, partially obstructing his vision and, with a big smile, picked her up.

"If you're a good girl, I'm going to treat you to some ice cream. What do you say?"

"You did not answer me. What are you plotting?"

"You insolent girl, don't you want ice cream?"

"Yes, I want!" answered the girl, in a loud voice.

"You must promise me that you'll always be good. Not just now, also tonight, when it's time to brush your teeth and go to bed, and tomorrow morning, when you have to get up and go to the kindergarten. You must always be good."

"Ugh! Do you buy the ice cream for me? "

"Sure. How many flavours? "

"Three: cream, milk cream, and chocolate!"

"You always get those. Don't you want to try some fruity flavours?"

"No! I don't like it. I want cream, milk cream, and chocolate!"

"Ok, ok. I'll ask mom if I can go get it now or after dinner."

"No, no! I want it now. Now! Come closer, I tell you something in your ear."

"Tell me."

"If you go… won't… promise."

"What did you say?" asked Kristian, who hadn't caught a word of what his sister had mumbled in his ear.

"Go now! We do not say anything to mom, I'll cover for you!" screamed impatiently the young girl.

"What? But, Darina! You shouldn't say such things. Especially, not while also shouting in my ears! I'm totally deaf, now."

The little scamp started whimpering. Her brother promised her ice cream, and now she wanted it.

"Don't make promises you can't keep," scolded him lightly his father, who'd silently witnessed the whole scene, standing by the door of Kristian's room. "Dinner's ready. Do not worry duckie: after you eat all your food, your brother will go get your ice-cream."

Darina was not happy with that solution at all, but she knew that if she'd played up for her ice-cream, her parents' reaction would be to decide not to indulge her with it at all. She made her brother put her on the ground, wiped her nose with a sleeve of her red t-shirt, for which both his father and older brother scolded her, then ran downstairs as fast as she could. Only a stupid dinner came between her and her ice cream, now. The father invited Kristian to follow his sister, as everyone was waiting for them to start the family meal.

After dinner, the boy went out to the ice-cream parlour next to the park, not far from home. Before going for the ice-cream, he went to make sure everything was in place. To set in motion the plan he'd been orchestrating for so many months, he'd bought a cell phone with a different number and created a new profile for all the social media he used to connect with the people of the Village. He'd found through the net some people who would help him reach the Village in Donegal, Ireland. From Varna, Bulgaria, a tourist town overlooking the Black Sea and surrounded by the waters of the homonymous lake, he planned to reach Sofia by car, then he'd board a plane to London. It would be a trip full of obstacles, and since he was still a minor, it wouldn't have been possible for him to take it alone. For about a year he'd saved all the pocket money he'd received from his parents and all the tips that the neighbours had given him for the odd jobs he made for them. He cleaned stairs, walked dogs, carried shopping bags, washed cars and all kinds of other stuff. That had gained him a decent amount of money, just enough to make his crazy dream come true. He knew it wasn't fair to his loving parents to leave his nest like that, like a fugitive, but they had left him no choice. Their attentions choked him, their retro ideas trapped him. He could not reproach them for anything but for loving him and his brother and sister too much. And he loved both his parents deeply in return, especially his mother. He knew that with that gesture he'd cut a huge wound in their hearts, but he would come back. He just needed some time to learn what he had to know, and then he'd come back. He knew they would've never let him leave, there wouldn't even be any kind of dialogue on the matter. He must finish secondary school first. Then, perhaps, they would talk about it. But the boy's impatience urged him to act rashly. He wanted to change the world, starting with his Country. Who better than the people of the Village to provide him with the right tools to make that dream come true? Two more years seemed just too long. He was afraid of losing that enthusiasm. What he didn't know, being so young, was that when a desire comes from the heart, as it did – that was out of the question – in two years his passion would only grow, encouraging him to pursue and realize his dreams. But he was only seventeen: he had to go and do everything right away, or the world would fall. And in some respects, he wasn't entirely wrong. Blessed unconscious youth.

***

James spent the whole night pondering. The two friends of the editor in chief had invited him to visit the Skulls in York, to get better acquainted with them, to learn who the blue-eyed man was and, why not, to join their covenant – as they defined it – even though that adjective didn't sound very good to the young journalist's ears. Everything was strange. Strange were the inhabitants of the Village in Donegal, strange the editor in chief's friends, and they both professed themselves as Celts. The first ones seemed to be a mix of people of different and distant cultures who had chosen to reunite under that ancient, historical and profoundly meaningful name. The Skull's pursued the same culture but limited it to it's purest, original, historical emanations, even though the Celts had little history. What James didn't understand, which intrigued him, was the reason for the explosive feelings between the two sides. Some kind of interest made so many people live in such a different way from everyone else – though the Celts of the Village were a numerous clan, while the Skull's of York seemed an exclusive club, to which only very few were allowed to join. All his thinking wouldn't find a way to solve the matters of his heart. The girl he'd been dating for the last three years, with whom he thought he'd established a relationship that, according to his imaginative projects, would have blossomed soon into a beautiful marriage, wanted nothing to do with him any longer. After hearing from the policeman that his boyfriend spent his nights in gay bars, any attempt at an approach on James' part had gone extremely wrong. To the girl, the word of a policeman could not in any way be questioned. She'd told him that, if he wanted a chance at renewing their relationship, they'd have to go see a shrink first. It was her right to know whether her boyfriend preferred her or strange men met in random clubs, and he needed to straighten up the confusion he most evidently was in. The young woman wouldn't hear reason. He'd tried to explain to her that it was all a huge misunderstanding, but she had left him no alternative. She was blocking his attempts to contact her on all sides: she deleted his number, blocked him in social networks, she even tried to block him out of her own thoughts, something she didn't seem to be able to do. Knowing he could not solve the situation in just a few days, James made a decision. "The dice is cast," he thought, as he planned his trip to the Skull's headquarters in York. The journey wouldn't take long, a couple of days at most. He packed throwing random stuff in his hand baggage, made a couple of phone calls to warn his colleagues that he wouldn't go to work the following days. The editor in chief replied:

"Go, go. Don't worry. The newspaper won't skip an issue for your absence."

After speaking to the editor in chief, James took a cab to the airport. It was only upon reaching the check-in, that he realized his day of departure hadn't come yet. A dark despair overtook him and he sadly took a cab back home.

***

Arkon, the guardian of the Haunted Forest, was not crazy about the horrid noise, as he liked to call it. He was more inclined to the sweet sounds of violins and harps, maybe accompanied by the voice of a soloist who could reach the highest notes, those infinite universal notes that merge delicately with the antimatter of space in the infinite void between one star and the other. Breton, on his part, adored that folkloristic music, and when he heard the notes in the distance he decided to use them as an excuse to visit his friend. The two spent their evenings talking about music, plants, stars, animals, the secrets of those places they guarded and the uncertain future, part of which was known to them. On music, they had different opinions, but both agreed that sooner or later an enlightened human would finally add a sixth line to the pentagram, introducing those two notes still unknown to the humans but very well known to everyone else: the Bi and the Di, after the Si. When this would happen, music would morph utterly, beginning a new era that would remain in the history of humanity until the end of time.

"Music is like an alphabet. We need twenty-six letters to communicate and those humans think that seven notes can be enough to play. How far they still need to go. Will we live on to see all this?"

"I don't know about you, I intend to!" answered Arkon, impertinently.

The party was at its climax – music covered every conversation – when an unbearable, shrill, overwhelming screelch filled the air. The High Priest

was startled. It took him a moment to understand, then he shouted:
"The curlicat! Beware of the curlicat!"

But it was too late, for when the curlicat screelched, at the same moment it fired his stinging quills. Charlie was already on the ground curled up in pain, and so were half of his band and a dozen other players and dancers. The second screelch was even more damaging: then it shot the microscopic quills of its long spindly tail.

"Iiiiiiihhhhhh!"

"Damn it, where's that filthy animal?" the High Priest lashed out, while another twenty people fell on the ground complaining of the pain.

"He's running towards the forest!" shouted Lyon, who saw something scatter in the dark towards the outskirts of the Village.

"I know who sent it. Tomorrow he's going to hear from me!" muttered the old man, while behind him another curlicat was about to cry out his first screelch.

"Careful! There's another one behind you."

The old man crouched just in time as the animal, seeing the human leap, frightened to death, followed his companion into the darkness.

"Arkon! I know you can hear me. Tomorrow we'll settle this."

"What have you done, why's the old man cross with you?"

"Nothing, nothing to worry about."

"You don't fool me. What did you do?"

"I sent him a couple of friends. That noise was terrible. I had to stop them!"

"You rascal. And you think he didn't recognize those screelches? I hope, for your sake, that he won't be as cross as to come and complain by me, or even worse by the Spring. You know They are vindictive and won't listen to reason."

"For a couple of quills? You're making it bigger than it is."

"The quills of the curlicat are extremely painful, and the smaller ones are not easy to remove. Look. They are returning to their nests… poor animals."

"Eheheh… Too bad I couldn't enjoy the show."

"I hope the Ancient Spirits of the Spring will discipline you once and for all!"

"Ugh. Spoilsports! It was just a harmless trick."

"You think? Do you see that light over there? The Spring is lighting up already. Don't you know what that means?"

Breton didn't have time to finish, Arkon had already disappeared. He knew that he'd gone too far this time, and he sure as hell didn't want to be caught. He knew that the Ancient Spirits were all but kind and that for his naughtiness he risked severe punishment. Meanwhile, in the Village, everyone who'd got past the attack unscathed was now helping the unfortunate hit removing the painful quills.

160

"What a welcome! I bet it was that spiteful Arkon," complained Charlie.

"Who else? I believe this time it was the music we played, that was not to his liking... but tomorrow we'll see what's what."

"Forget it. What can you do to him, anyway?"

"Me, probably nothing. But I know someone who can."

The Great High Priestess had summoned the High Priestess of the Elm to the holy tent.
"What must I do to get some peace? I asked for some collaboration from all of you, in order to be allowed to question the Gods for the problem you already know. I don't think I've asked for too much. What's all this hubbub?"

"The Scottish brothers have arrived for our yearly gathering."

"Yes, yes. I know. And along with them comes their noise. But what's with all this turmoil?"

"A pair of curlicats shot quills and everyone panicked..."

"I must trust you to handle the situation. I am asking you, please, to allow me all the concentration I need to pray. Kindly remind our guests and our own to respect my will. I am the Great High Priestess, what the heck! I demand that you take action. Beginning with your husband, who is the worst of them all!"

The High Priestess of the Elm came out of the tent visibly worried and the first person she met was her husband.

"Honey, honey. We would really need a little ointment..."

"You, go home without another word!" said her in a decisive tone.

"But..."

The High Priestess only needed a stern look to silence him. He went home and she went to the infirmary to send away all those who didn't need treatment, recommending them to be silent on their way home. She then took the situation into her own hands and took care of everyone injured, in absolute silence.

"What happened?" Ryan asked in a whisper to the High Priest of the Elm, whom he met in the middle of the road. The old man slowly brought the index finger of his right hand to his mouth. As the boy's mother and sister arrived, a nod from the woman was enough to make Ryan desist from asking anything else and follow her.

It was late into the night when the High Priestess of the Elm finally came home.
"Is everything all right?"

"Yes, everyone's in bed. And instead of trying to help me, you'd rather be the leader of the ruckus…"

"What have I done? We were celebrating. You were having fun, too."

"Yes, yes. You always have the best excuses. You should be the one to set a good example, instead, you'll party as hard as anyone else!"

"Is it because of the old caryatid? Did she complain?"

"Do not call her so. It is she who governs here."

"I don't mean to be disrespectful, but she's over ninety years old… she is not so young anymore."

"The teenager's talking! You know what, let's go to sleep. We'll talk about it tomorrow."

***

It was late at night when Kristian tiptoed into action. He took only the strictly necessary, then went to the front door. But he wasn't the only one awake that night. His brother Nikolai wasn't asleep and saw him walking by the door of his room. For a moment, he was tempted to call his older brother. However, despite his young age of fourteen, he understood what was going on with him. For months now, he'd been discussing, quarrelling, and squabbling whenever his parents were in the house. Mom and dad were exasperated. Kristian seemed to have been exchanged with an alien from another planet. He spent his days wandering around the city, often ending up at the necropolis by the lake, where he spent hours trying to identify himself with the population that lived in those lands almost seven thousand years ago. It was a numerous tribe, judging from the size of the necropolis, extending over an area of about 7,500 square meters. It was evident from the large number – almost three hundred – of graves found, and the numerous gold objects that decorated the bodies found in forty of those tombs. Whenever his mother sent him to look for his brother, Nikolai found him there. And they argued every time he had to convince him to come back home. Sometimes they fought so much they ended up beating each other up: those were the times when it didn't end very well for Nikolai. Kristian always managed to earn his brother's forgiveness, as they loved each other so much, but it seemed clear that the house was feeling too small to him. His People called to him. He had a mission to accomplish and it couldn't wait a day longer. He felt sure in his heart that his People needed to get back their own lives, taking its distance from the ideological slavery that had isolated it from the world for half a century and also from the Western enslavement that was crushing it, deluding it with a fake sense of freedom. He needed to immerse himself in his own roots, those of the great free People who inhabited the land he lived in, thousands of years ago. The situation was perfectly clear to Nikolai: Kristian was running away and for all he loved him, as he shared some of his ideas he decided to shut up and turn away, muffling his sighs. Kristian heard him anyway, stopped in mid-motion, took a step back and looked from the doorframe. Seeing his brother asleep, he felt a lump in his throat, and he came almost to the point of going back to bed and stop that folly. He stood there for a few moments, observing his brother, a solitary tear sliding down his right cheek. Then he collected himself. He was convinced that what he was doing would do good to his brothers, too. He returned to the corridor, listened to the quiet of the house at night, then he went down the stairs. He left a note, a few lines he'd written the evening before, on the table in the kitchen.

"Forgive me, I really must go.
I promise I'll be safe and, as soon as I'm ready, I'll come back.

I love you all,
Kristian"
Silently, he went to the front door. He took the key out of the lock and, making as little noise as possible, opened the door and closed it behind him. He tiptoed down the first flight of stairs, then the second, the third, until he reached the front door. At last, he was out: his long journey to the Donegal Village was finally begun. Kristian had worn his favourite – strictly black and grey – clothes and comfortable black, grey and brown sneakers, with white stripes and bi-coloured strings. The right shoe with a black string, the left shoe with a white one. He had to reach his school, a friend from school would be waiting for

him there. Petrov, that was his name, was always looking for easy money. Kristian had persuaded him to drive him to Sofia in secret for a hundred Lev, in exchange for this sum he'd also made him promise never to say a word of it to anyone.
Petrov was waiting for him with his red Lada Nive, a ramshackle off-road vehicle they would drive on a 450 Km journey that night.

"Finally! I was about to leave."

"You wouldn't have. I haven't paid you yet. Come on now, let's go."

"You made me wait half an hour, and now you're in a hurry? You wouldn't be running away, would you?" said the older boy with evident sarcasm, while he climbed awkwardly, hampered by his weight, into the car.

"Do you have the money?"

"Sure."

"Give it, then."

"We said I'd pay you in Sofia."

"Come on, I need to fill up the tank!"

"That wasn't part of our deal!"

"Oh crap! If you'd rather go on foot, be my guest. Come on, just give me a half!"

Kristian did not like to compromise: he'd always be true to his word and he expected others to do the same. But he had no alternative. He gave Petrov 30 Lev, complaining that everything was not alright since the original agreement wasn't being abided by.

"Just stop it. If it wasn't for me, you wouldn't reach your friend in Sofia at all."

"Can we leave already?" asked Kristian annoyed.

"Alright, alright. Let's go, then. If I can get the car going, that is," answered Petrov in an uncertain tone. Starting the engine on that car always seemed to be a problem.

***

The next morning James got up very early, even though he'd already packed his suitcase the day before. After shaving and taking a refreshing shower, he had a quick breakfast: long black coffee one sugar, two rusks, one with peanut butter, the other with blackberry jam. On his bed, he had prepared the clothes he wanted to wear: a pair of jeans, a casual shirt, medium-heeled black shoes, dark blue socks, a creamy spring jacket, cut out like a suit jacket but with a zipper. He was ready to go, with his London fog suitcase, with all he needed for his upcoming three-days journey. Before leaving, he went to the bathroom to brush his teeth and carefully combed his hair. He parted it on the left and styled a lock to fall down over his right eye without covering it with a touch of gel-lacquer. He was done and ready to leave. Almost. Before leaving, even if he didn't have to – his mother had taught him this when he was a child – he would try and sit on the toilet for any last minute physiological need. Done that, he washed his hands with the dark green liquid Aleppo soap he kept on the sink, which had a pungent fragrance, not necessarily pleasant, but that he loved so much. A splash of 'Obsession', in an attempt to hide the smell of soap, and off he went. Upon leaving, he checked for all the lights to be turned off: bathroom, bedroom, corridor, living room. He closed all the shutters and glass windows, turned off the gas tap and the electricity. He took his keys and a bag where he'd collected some leftover non-durable food from the fridge to leave in front of the neighbour's door. During the three days of his absence, it would've gone bad, while the old neighbour could have enjoyed it instead. With the poor retirement she lived on, James had seen her several times rummaging into the dumpster behind the supermarket around the corner, looking for some salad or some packaged or canned good just barely past its expiration date. It was not the first time he had done that, he always did it when he knew he wouldn't eat some of the food he'd bought. He didn't have loads of money to waste, but he didn't cheap out on food, nor was he particularly prone to comply with any strict dietary rules. However, he just couldn't stand the idea of wasting food. He locked the door behind him, hanged the food's bag to the neighbour's door, and went downstairs. The cab he'd called for awaited him by the sidewalk. He got in and asked the driver to take him to the airport.

"No suitcase?" asked the driver back, as he got the meter running. James mumbled something, got out of the cab, ran up the stairs, and entered his home, all to retrieve the suitcase he'd left in the bedroom. Once he got back on the stairwell, he couldn't help but notice that the bag hanging on the neighbour's door was empty already. He retrieved it, went back to his apartment, tried to turn on the light, however as he'd disconnected the main switch it wouldn't. He cursed against unlikely existing beings, then rushed to get the light back on. He entered the bedroom, hoking his jacket into the handle, and tearing it off. He then ran to the closet, threw everything out, frantically searching for a similar jacket, which he didn't have. He decided he would just buy another one as soon as he arrived in London. He wanted to put everything back, but as he looked around at the mess that he'd made, he realized that he'd need more than an hour to clean it all out. He kept on ranting at everything, left it all as it was and switched off the bedroom light. He then went to the bathroom for a last minute pee, washed his hands with the liquid Aleppo soap, ran to the door, turn off the electricity, closed the door behind him, taking care to turn the armoured locks as well and run down the stairs. Halfway through the second flight, a terrible doubt nagged him: had he shut the electricity off? And what about the gas? Puffing and panting and ranting against the world, he retraced his steps, as the door of his old neighbour shut suddenly right on his face. He had no time to think about her. He unlocked the door and went to switch on the light to check the gas handle. Once he'd realized that everything was in fact all right, he was finally ready to leave. But, before he went out, he had to go to the bathroom. He dropped his suitcase in the corridor, ran to the bathroom, tried – quite unsuccessfully – to pee, washed his hands with the liquid Aleppo soap, just because. The pungent smell of the soap was beginning to nauseate him. He switched off the bathroom light, grabbed his suitcase, turned off the light in the corridor, checked if the gas tap was closed, turned off the main switches, closed and locked the front door, while his nosy neighbour's shut close again. He muttered something insulting towards the old woman, loudly giggling behind her own door at the mess her neighbour was making, upon which she'd spied from her peephole since the very beginning. James finished to lock the door and rushed down the stairs. He climbed back into the cab, noticing that the meter already signed ten euros for the ride he hadn't yet taken to the airport of Dublin. Finally, the cab moved. But it would have been too simple. About ten minutes into the ride, as he was going over everything he had to do and to take before he left, he realized that he'd forgotten his wallet home. He began to feel his back pockets, especially the right one, where he usually kept it. He couldn't believe how distracted he'd been the whole morning. He looked for it over and over, but it was all in vain. The wallet, with his documents, the money, and the credit cards, was at home, in the trousers he was wearing the day before.

"Lost something?" asked the cab driver, looking at his client in the rearview mirror, while James, furious at best, was mentally loathing and insulting himself with the most brutal vexations he'd ever thought of.

"We must go back."

"Are you sure? You risk missing your plane."

"Well, I don't think I am going anywhere without a wallet, anyway," answered James reluctantly, still mentally insulting himself.

The cab driver managed to refrain a sarcastic smile. He turned around the car and returned to the address where that mindless man lived. James jolted down the cab, almost got mowed by the passing cars, which began to be numerous because the time was approaching when everyone went to work or school. When he got to his building he saw that all the old spinsters and widows were by their windows. Watching the people who ran to get to work or school, with all it ensued, was their favourite pastime. All that commotion amused them, especially when a small crash happened, a car didn't give way, a car driver insulted the tram driver when he couldn't manage to surpass it. He could see them, guffawing at his misfortunes.

He ran up the stairs, unlocked the door, entered the apartment, turned on the electricity, and went straight to the bedroom, trying to find the pants from the day before in all the chaos he'd made when looking for the jacket. After almost a quarter of an hour of searching and ranting, he suddenly remembered that he'd undressed in the living room, the night before. And there they were, leaning on the back of the sofa, the wallet visibly poking out of the back pocket. James drew a sigh of relief, but all the rage and angst took their toll on his stomach, and the coffee he'd drunk for breakfast was starting to take effect. To the bathroom he went – whatever, he would have gone anyway. Once the contents of his bowels were evacuated, he washed his hands with the liquid Aleppo soap. Upon drying them, an atrocious doubt nagged him: had he taken the last pee? He tried, and again nothing came out of his bladder. He rinsed his hands again with the liquid Aleppo soap and off he went. He switched off the bathroom light, the bedroom light, the corridor light, the kitchen light – after checking on the gas handle – the living room light, and electricity. He closed and locked the entrance door to the very last turn of the key while hearing the old caryatid laughing at him behind her peephole. "Damned nosy old bat!" James ranted out in his head and ran down the stairs.

Once in the street, he couldn't see the cab anymore, so he started to look for it going backward in the one-way street. Observing the clumsiness of his client, the cab driver began to honk the horn. The timing wasn't the best, though: the commotion generated by the traffic was deafening, and many a horn honked in response. After five minutes of fruitless search, just when James had finally taken his cell phone to call the cab, he saw one of the neighbours calling out to him from a window:
"Kid? Excuse me! Hey, lad!"

James, furious and embarrassed, pretended not to hear.

"Young man! Eheheh. Look! Your cab's over there, across the street. Eheheh. Just there, where you left it!"

James looked up, and there it was, just across the street from him, the cab driver honking and flailing his arms all over. He cursed under his breath, then waved back and, finally, he turned to the old woman who had helped him to thank her, but by then she could barely breathe, she was having so much fun. Not to mention the others. Some even felt lightheaded, they were laughing so hard. Crossing the road was another adventure for James. He spent five minutes trying to cross and almost ending up run down by a couple on a motorbike, a nun on a bicycle, three boys on scooters and the tram driver, who hit hard on his brakes and still barely managed to stop a half inch from James' body, threatening to run him down on purpose if he'd try a stunt like that again. James had to return to the sidewalk, hearing behind him the old unpleasant neighbours, all cheering the tram driver for his excellent driving skills. The boys on the tram didn't refrain from ranting against James as well since the sudden stop of the vehicle had dropped them on their knees. As if it wasn't enough, he stayed on watching at James and daring him to try and cross the street again before he'd left. "Damn it," sworn the young journalist under his breath. At last, he managed to cross the street and get on the cab, which by now signed a bill of 30 euros for the drive to the airport he still hadn't begun. The cab driver wouldn't say a word, James ordered him to the airport and they finally left.

***

It was dawn, and Ildegard had not been able to sleep that night. Her family was hosting the daughter of the Scottish guitarist of Charlie's band, who had the same age as her, and with whom she'd been talking the whole entire night. Having their Scottish friends at the Village had caused great excitement to everyone. The girls stood by the window, side by side, commenting on the beauty of the landscape as the first rays of the sun shone in the morning sky. Then Ildegard saw in the distance the High Priest of the Elm walking towards the Haunted Forest. She'd waited so long to ask him to bring her with him to one of those walks, so, together with her friend, she quickly got dressed and rushed down the stairs. They hadn't reached the front door yet, when Ildegard's father, Ubert, called them back:
"Where do you think you're going, the two of you?"

"We saw the High Priest, he is going to the Haunted Forest, maybe even to the Spring! I really want to go with him…"

"Ildegard! Even if it were true, and the High Priest of the Elm was going to the Spring, I don't think he'd like to have your company in this particular instance. He'd have left at a more suitable time otherwise, don't you agree? Now, since it isn't five o'clock yet, shouldn't two girls of your age still be in bed, dreaming of unicorns and all magical things?"

"Ugh! Can we at least say hello?"

"What are you two doing, there? Get back to your beds fast as light, or else!" intervened the girl's mother, a little less diplomatic than her father was, at five in the morning.

"What's all the hubbub?" mumbled Ryan stepping out of his bedroom all disheveled and still in his pyjamas.
The Scottish girl became tomato-red, while everybody pretended not to notice her.

"Ryan, you too, back to bed," told him his father.

"I would love to. In fact, I'd still be there if someone hadn't been screaming in the corridor, right in front of my door!"

"Alright, that's it. Everyone in bed!" sentenced the mother, pointing towards the kids' rooms.

"Why are the two of you still out here?" added the father, gently pushing the girls to their room.

"Don't tell me you like my brother?"

"No! It's just… How can I put it? I don't know… He's cute."

"Who, Hatchet Face?"

"Stop it, you know it's not true. He was all sleepy, ruffled, and still in his pyjamas… He was just… He's really sweet and cute."

"Sweet? Cute? Yuck. My brother is not sweet at all. Don't tell me you're one of those who'll just fall for any boy she sees?"

"Don't be so stern! I just said I find him nice."

"Come on, let's go to sleep. Perhaps after some rest, you'll come back to your senses and you'll see how my brother really is. Moreover, he's engaged already…"

"Yes, I know. He's with Brenda. I can't compete with her, for sure. He will never see me."

"Hey! Hey! You're speaking like you're in love, now. Let's go to sleep," said Ildegard, taking her friend by the arm and rolling her eyes.

She followed her friend to bed, but her eyes were wide open, as she tried to commit to mind the image of Ildegard's brother with his eyes half-closed and frowning, still ruffled and visibly sleepy, and with that pyjama showcasing his beautiful body. An angel. She wondered, what if she could have rested her ear to his heart, to hear it beating. She dreamed of him in her young head.

Ildegard wasn't asleep either, the girl was lost in her own thoughts, but her weren't for the boy in the next room. He hadn't come with Charlie's clan. Yet, his grandfather had told her that a foreign boy would arrive that summer to stay for the rest of his life and that they would be together. Of course, it seemed an incredible story, but the annual autumnal meeting in which the High Priestesses interrogated the oracles for the following year, had communicated this particular episode that concerned the youngest of the Orion family. Her grandfather wasn't able to resist his niece's insistence and revealed her one of the secrets of that meeting. For this, he'd been severely rebuked by the Great High Priestess and the High Priestess of the Elm. For six months he'd been given extra chores. Light ones, of course, nothing that would hurt him with his venerable age and all. However, he never regretted spilling the beans to Ildegard. He doted for his niece and he saw nothing wrong with what he'd done. He knew that Ildegard would easily become a High Priestess when her time came since she possessed all the necessary skills to rise in the hierarchy. At the moment, the only issue was her young age. But even so, she was already as mature, if not even more, as many older girls already advancing on the long road that would lead them to become priestesses and, maybe, one day, High Priestesses.

Meanwhile, the High Priest of the Elm was crossing the border of the Village. After passing the bridge on the canal surrounding the town, he heard someone calling his name. He turned and saw his friend Charlie walking towards him, waving.

"What are you doing up at this ungodly hour?" he asked, curiously.

"I have something to say to your friend. The joke he pulled on us yesterday wasn't nice at all."

"You won't find him, he's long gone. I am going to the Spring, to ask that he gets what he's due. There will be consequences, you'll see."

"I'll go with you."

"Are you sure? It's a long walk."

"Hey, I'm still fit, you know?"

"Fit? Like, you'd fit into a beer barrel, you mean?"

The two went on, laughing and joking at and with each other. They'd known each other for a very long time, and they shared a great friendship. The journey into the Haunted Forest became a journey through their shared memories of their previous times together. Then they reached the Plane's Grove and stopped by the ruins to drink a sip of water and lit a campfire to make some coffee.

"Do you remember that time we decided we had to sing here?"

"Of course, I remember. The Great High Priestess had us locked up in the library, to prevent it."

"Well, even if we didn't get to do that, we sure had a lot of fun that year."

"We were so mean to the poor old woman. My wife didn't speak to me for two months, after that. And the priestess punished me into next year! But I regret nothing of it. Nothing at all."

"Well, replacing the ceremonial book with Aesop's fables wasn't the nicest thing…"

"Eheheh, it's not my fault that she doesn't even know what she's reading from during the ritual."

"And what about that other time, when we replaced the olive oil with petrol?"

"If only she'd had any sense of smell at all…"

The two kept on fishing for all the merry memories of their past. After a half hour, they resumed their journey towards the Sacred Wood, at the centre of which lay the Sacred Spring.

"How far we've come since we met for the first time," exclaimed Charlie when they finally were in front of the Source, as he patted the High Priest of the Elm on the back.

"And how far do we have to go, still."

"I think it's time for us to calm down, Gregorian. As they say: make way for the young."

"Give them all the way you want, but let's not forget us old wise men, eheheh!"

"Wise? You, maybe. You are a Druid. But me? I've got nothing but good lungs. Well, good enough to play my bagpipe."

"Charlie, knowing how to play is one of the most beautiful gifts we can pass on to future generations. If you are not a wise man, who is? Breton? Breton! Are you there?"

"We might have known. One has run away to hide, and the other doesn't want to meddle."

"You know, I think you're right. But I'll take care of that prankster of Arkon, now," said the High Priest of the Elm, throwing some ashes he'd brought in a terracotta vase, into the heart of the Spring. The ashes were what was left of the episode that had happened the night before. It was a very serious matter, as it had bothered the villagers, but more importantly, as it had involved honoured guests and visitors from the outside. Seen the discomfort and minor physical damages that it had entailed, the High Priests of the Village performed a ritual to beg the spiritual entities of the Spring to discipline the culprit, identified in the warden spirit of the Haunted Forest, Arkon. The ritual, held in the Sacred Tent by the High Priestess of the Elm, consisted of writing the incident and the name of the culprit on a piece of parchment. Meanwhile, the purest incenses were mixed together and fumigated: three grains of olibanum, two of myrrh and one of the more acidulous benzoin. Once the incident was written using some ink dedicated to Saturn's sphere, the parchment was burned on the coal where the incense was previously fumigated, to imprint the contents of the parchment in the element of air. It was an elemental ritual in which the four basic elements of the Earth played a key role, as the great alchemists taught in the Middle Ages: Earth was represented by the parchment, Water by the ink, Fire by the coal, and smoke represented Air. Through this ritual, events could be communicated to the Elemental Spirits of the Avatar.

Only them – if they'd deem it opportune – could punish the responsible of the mischief.
When the ashes touched the surface of the water, the Spring interrupted its flow. Some time later the water poured out again: the Elemental Spirits had examined the events and decided what to do. Because the perpetrator was a guardian and a spirit, the villagers would never know the decision of the Spring, but the High Priests were sure that exemplary punishment would be brought upon the Guardian of the Haunted Forest. The two friends thanked the Gods and set off for the Village. If they'd walk fast enough, they'd arrive just in time for lunch.

End of Episode 03

Episode 04
ADELE

She sat in her kitchen by the window, but the fixedness of her gaze betrayed her: if anyone could have seen her, they would have realized immediately that she wasn't looking at the lawn outside.
From time to time she looked away, blinking, annoyed by her own reflection in the shiny, spotless window glass. The front lawn of her detached house, bare of even the smallest of trees, allowed a wide view on the road, only bounded by the low hedges which bordered it on both sides, separating her from the rest of the world. The green was meticulously kept to give off the impression that a happy family lived within those walls, but it was not the case.
Her eyes peered into the sky, at that time of the year of a brilliant blue, a colour far removed from her state of mind, looking for a shred of serenity in the warmth of that spring afternoon. She searched her mind for a memory to hold on to, one that would distract her from her worries. Shortly thereafter, she realized that she was looking at the floor. The thoughts that obsessed her always brought her forcefully back to the reality she lived in. Becoming aware of the shapes and colours of her kitchen floor, she raised her head once more, towards the street over the edge of her garden. She saw the noisy cars parade one after the other in the distance, they were

out of focus, almost transparent as sudden shadows of speed and colour.

She made a list in her mind of all the things she had to do before the night came.

She had no time to waste, although… She didn't know what to do, her mind becoming fuzzier and fuzzier as always when confronted with a decision. Whatever she chose to do wouldn't change a thing, anyway. Her back was in constant pain, she couldn't remember whether it was due to an accidental fall or a blow, one of many she'd received. If only… If only she'd had somewhere else to go, if only she'd had the courage – the strength – to run away, flee, leave… She couldn't count the times she'd thought to do it. But she couldn't. She didn't know how, nor felt strong enough to do it. And therefore she suffered.

She exhaled slowly closing her eyes, and with that deep sight, a tear rolled down her cheek, with excruciating slowness.

Even crying had become difficult.

She opened her eyes and her eyelids fluttered one, two, three times. Then, she brought her right hand to her cheek and gently wiped the drop from her cheek with her fingertips, as if to give herself a caress.

She missed those little tender gestures, those sweet attentions, those moments of love she hadn't experienced for so long, she had almost forgotten. So long was past since someone had deigned her with a single gentle look or affectionate gesture.

But moving her arm she couldn't hold back a lament caused by the pain she felt spreading from the purple bruise shining just over her shoulder, well hidden under the dress she was wearing.

What about dinner? What had he instructed her to prepare? Oh, right, she remembered. And how could she have forgotten about it? But lost in the haze of her dreamlike thoughts, she had a habit to repeat everything he told her, from time to time, for fear of making mistakes.

In the past, she had tried anything, but by now, she had lost all hope. She'd stayed because she was sure things could change if only she would commit. She'd stayed because she'd wanted to commit. But although she had, nothing had changed. She'd ended up losing everything. Her self-esteem, the strength to go on, the stubbornness to never give up. But above all, she had lost her love. She was no longer able to love. She still tried, sometimes, desperately and with all her strength, to love the only reason that forced her to suffer in silence for all those years. But her efforts weren't rewarded. The creature she had brought into the world was made of the same stuff as the one who'd reduced her in that state.

She couldn't bear the idea of having brought another monster into the world. She had lost her peace to it. She couldn't understand.

All the times she thought she'd been abandoned, all the times she'd wanted to give up and cry, she kept repeating to herself how fate had been unfair to her. But in the end, she knew she was the only one she should be angry with. She should have given up long ago. But her young age had betrayed her, and she'd deluded herself that she would be able to shape that person, her one true love, with whom she'd decided to dedicate her life to.

The results of her efforts had only been harassment. Her stubbornness, progressively nullified by brutality. Her life-force diminished every passing day, depriving her of the sharpness of mind that would allow her to make different, braver and less painful choices.

And again, the creamy-brown tiled floor, with its white flowers and the almost imperceptible yellow pistils, returned to the centre of her eyes. How painful and tiring it was, raising her delicate face time and time again. With a laconic expression, hampered by her fleeting exhaustion, she tried to rest her head on her left hand. But it couldn't last long: the haematoma that enveloped her elbow wasn't completely dissipated yet. It had been two months since that particular beating. She was beginning to think that maybe something could have been broken. Perhaps a badly re-calcified micro-fracture. In any case, it hurt.

She stretched out her arm and flexed it. That movement, if performed delicately enough and only to some extent, gave her a momentary relief. If she moved too much though, the pain would sharply bring her back to the moment when the wound was inflicted on her. She'd never hurt herself, on purpose or else. Although her parents were severe, she couldn't remember similar episodes from her childhood, either. She squinted, trying to deal with a terrible headache that was tormenting her. The effort was futile, the headache wouldn't go away unless she took a painkiller. This, too, had never happened to her before. For this, she'd been going to the doctor, without result. At every appointment, the doctor would suggest that she took specialistic tests, but they were expensive, and she wasn't worth spending money on. Every time she would complain, the headache would get stronger. It came in such strong shocks that led her to think that her brain wanted to escape that container, so terribly mistreated. Another tear fell, this time down her left cheek. With a handkerchief she kept in the pocket of her blue and white striped apron, she wiped it from her chin with a graceful, gentle upwards movement. Once the handkerchief was back in the pocket, she gave up another anguished sigh.

A billion thoughts overlapped in her mind. She wanted to act, ached to do something, but she didn't know where to start, how to react, what to do that wouldn't end up in another painful submission. Nothing. All those ideas seemed crazy. Any solution, impractical. All her fragile hopes wrecked against the cliff of her despair consumed yet reinforced and solidified by the countless waves of all the mistreatments she'd suffered. Nothing lay on her horizon. Everywhere she looked, she could see that miserable flatness that was her life, surrounded by nests of cockroaches, without any distractions. Without even a glimmer of hope to make her smile on that warm spring afternoon. It was hard to resist to such desolate despair for so long. The right hemisphere of her brain, the unconscious part no one can control, although in the waves of pain, produced soft, warm, happy thoughts as if to defend her and itself from all that.

She was stubborn, resolute, her inner strength was the only thing that had allowed her to survive her sad situation. The most beautiful memories came from her youth. How could she ever forget that young boy who, once, stole her heart? A thin line sits on her face now, where once upon a time a smile would have exploded. Nothing more than a hint, the vestige of a muscular reflex from a time long lost. So slight, it would have been almost imperceptible to an inexperienced eye.

But that was the best she had, the expression of a shy happiness she now reserved only to those whose memories were truly close to her heart. Barely hinted, because he could not bear to know her happy. She could not afford to be happy in his presence, and even as she was sure of his absence, she still trembled at the fear that he might suddenly appear behind her, as it had happened one too many times before. She'd lost count of how many times that gesture of serenity had been clouded by his rebukes, her screams, his hits. Still, it wasn't enough. He'd instigate the other one against her, too. The one she insisted on calling her angel, the one she could not think of without feeling a burst of love, somewhere, deep down. Her motherly heart wouldn't give up on him. It didn't matter how many times she'd suffer because of the stories, the subterfuges and the lies that he'd tell the other one. He'd still be her little angel. Her own son. He couldn't really be blamed, she couldn't bear the idea of him being another responsible of her desolate damnation. He was unaware, he was too young, he lacked the malice that only adults possessed. He was nothing but her baby boy and although he was fifteen years old, she persisted in believing him innocent as when he was five. Her happiest memory, besides that of her son's birth, was the one of that young boy she'd once known in the village, when the village was but a dream, a project in the minds of a small community. She remembered when her parents had decided to join those bizarre people, with their bizarre habits, bizarre way of thinking, bizarre way of doing even the most common everyday things. Ways she liked so much. His father endured them less, but he'd still follow his wife, who'd become involved because of her sister, a close relative to the Great High Priestess. At home they wouldn't talk of anything else but of those people, of the new world that was about to begin, of the new philosophy that had to be sown and watched while it would grow. An extraordinary adventure to live with those people, who shared that bizarre way of life. When the three of them arrived to the Village, it was but a small group of five battered wooden huts. Partly it was because the High Priest of the Elm, the young man who'd built them, wasn't a very experienced contractor, partly because they happened to be among the first who arrived to the Village, to form that first community. He was already there. A clean face, a penetrating gaze, a thin mouth. She was immediately crazy for that young boy, and he reciprocated. How beautiful the life in the Village was. Her smile almost widened, but then, as if hit by an electric shock, she recomposed her face into a neutral mask. Her wandering gaze had stopped onto the clock on the wall, and she was trying to figure out whether it was too late or not. Then her gaze was pulled out of the window again, instantly captured by the oh so enviable freedom of a flock of black birds that crossed the sky above her house, disappearing from her sight. She couldn't fathom where they were going. "Blessed be their immense freedom," murmured her lost once again, in her hazy state. She still had some time.

If it were a different family, if she were a different woman, she would hardly have had more than five minutes to choke herself up with such futile, depressing, obsessive thoughts. If she'd had the opportunity to browse through a magazine, read a book, surf the net, chat with friends, or better yet, organize a relaxing afternoon of walking, drinking tea, going to the gym or playing whist with her friends, sure.

But she was not another woman. She was Adele. She was as sweet as that name she cursed. Truth be told, it wasn't the name itself that bothered her, it was herself. She'd come to hate herself so much, that she could barely bear to hear her own name. Her resentment was born from her lack of reaction, her greatest fault, for which she would never forgive herself.

He came back to mind. The sunset strolls along the path to the Haunted Forest, the first spats with the insolent Arkon, the tender effusions in the Plane's Grove, the races for a sip from the Spring at the centre of the Sacred Wood, and Breton reproaching them and then leaving them be. But they were not alone in that newborn community: there were about a dozen of boys and girls their age, and every day someone new arrived. The first version of the Sacred Tent, small and rudimentary, was the place where they welcomed the new arrivals. Everyone had a specific task for the day and every day they would receive a new one. Of course, anyone who ended up sweeping, washing dishes or doing the laundry for the day would complain, but they would do them all together, and her life with that group of crazy-heads was always incredibly light and fun. Granted, it was no Pleasure Island: every day there was something to discuss. The community was young and quarrels were a daily occurrence, but then someone always managed to bring back the calm and serenity. The only one who didn't seem to ever get accustomed to that way of life was her father, who felt like a fish out of water, always sulking, grumpy and unfriendly with her mother, who tried to act as a buffer between him and the other villagers. One of the strongest memories of that place was the dawn she woke up every morning to admire. She'd get up and she'd open the window of her small but cozy bedroom in the wooden house her family shared with other three. She also remembered with some nostalgia the green foliage of the trees, the songs of the birds, the warm sun in the blue sky and the smiles of the villagers. She would get up early with all the other young people of the community. Besides their daily tasks, they had planned sporting activities, breakfast together with the adults, study time with that somewhat pretentious professor who demanded commitment and dedication above all in the mnemonic technique, a prerogative of druids. If he hadn't been the father of his favourite, she wouldn't have devoted all that commitment to his classes, nor to the hours of library duty, she spent arranging those thousands of books that he kept receiving from all over the world. Then everyone went to perform their daily task. Some would prepare lunch, some would help to build new, sturdier homes, some would tend to the first lots of cultivated fields that, someday, would become the Village's Herbarium. And how to forget that loud American with her crazy plans for a huge greenhouse and botanical garden, always demanding more hands than the community could provide.

Those memories required total isolation, so Adele eventually ventured to close her eyes. At that moment her smile returned to her face, and tears flowed copiously.

"Damn!" exclaimed her, taking her handkerchief to wipe her face. "Damn it," repeated, feeling as if she were unworthy of such pleasant digressions. "Damn!"

She was always crying. Often for the pain, sometimes for depression, others for the desolation, and only very rarely for a happy memory.

And she was tired. So much so that even those few tears would drain all her energy.

She took a glimpse of the clock, just enough to make sure she still had time to wonder.

Her thoughts floated back to all those unrealistic ways she could have used to escape from her cage. Getting a job was a sore point. She had never been able to work, how would she maintain herself? At her age, who would have even considered to employ her? She was no longer young, and couldn't do a thing. Though not for lack of trying. But there never seemed to be a way. He wouldn't hear of that: she must take care of the house and he would work. A medieval mentality, quite anachronistic, but through that and many others, he had ensured her submission. Yes, that was the word. She depended on him to live. And he made her pay, pay and pay, every minute of every day, whenever he'd get the chance which, unfortunately, happened very often.

She still remembered very clearly the first time she'd tried to find a job. They had just moved to Camden and the bakery near the apartment they lived in was looking for a saleswoman. She'd read the sign when she'd gone out to buy some bread for his dinner. She'd immediately inquired after the open position, as she wanted to contribute to maintaining the family as her parents and her dear friends of the Village had taught her. The baker was immediately enthusiastic and gave her an appointment for the following morning. She'd come home happy and radiant, impatient to tell her loving husband how lucky she'd been to find employment so close to home. He immediately became gloomy and an argument arose. He insisted that she must worry about the baby she was carrying and that a good mother would never put her son's health at risk. She replied that she would

still be able to work without any contraindications for three or four months, even more, as she was at the very beginning of her pregnancy, and, above all, that her future employer, whom she'd immediately informed of the situation, had not posed an issue. The discussion went on until she burst into tears. He came to her, apologetic, for the one and only time she could remember of, and he whispered that he loved her so much that if that really was her wish, he wouldn't hinder her, no more. She calmed down, hugged him and cuddled until he left to go back to work. The following morning, Adele dressed carefully, to make a good impression. But when she arrived at the store, she had a bitter surprise. The shutter was closed, there was soot everywhere, a white and red delimitation tape, with a sheet, informing the people to stay away, as the place was being seized for an undergoing investigation. A little old man, shaking his head, murmured something incongruous. She approached him. "Poor man, and poor his wife and four young children, too. What a terrible, terrible tragedy…"
"Excuse me, sir? Do you know… Could you tell me… What happened?"

"Good morning, my dear. Don't you know?"

"Know what?"
"The bakery… it caught fire, during the night. And poor William…"

"William? You mean the baker?"

"Yes, yes. They found him still trapped inside. Charred."

"Oh my God! But… but how did it happen?"

"We don't know nothing, yet. Some electrical problem, maybe a short-circuit."

Adele went home upset, and upon his return, she told her husband what had happened to the bakery. He looked surprised and bewildered and hugged her commenting that she'd been really lucky, for if that incident would have happened but a few hours later, who knew what might have been of her. He held her hard and tight, whispering how sorry he was, and that he'd do everything he could to help her find another job. The following days, the newspapers wrote that – according to the police report – the baker had committed suicide and, even though some obscure points remained, the case had been closed. At first, she believed what she read, but as days, weeks, and months past, she'd start to ponder another possibility. The man had been killed by her husband. In time, she came to be entirely sure of this. However, unfortunately, she had no proof. That man's death fell on her, and she couldn't forgive herself for that.

Every time she remembered those times, she would repeat "Poor good man…"

That death weighed on her soul like a boulder hanging from her neck over the edge of a bottomless pit. She couldn't manage to make peace with it, although she'd paid dearly on her own skin for her suspicions first, and her knowledge then, of the homicide perpetrated by her husband, of which she still hadn't managed to obtain his confession to this day. No other job opportunity would come her way until his son reached the age of nursery school. By then she'd finally gained the courage to leave the house again. Just then, her husband's bans became even more strict. The threats came and the violence followed. At first, they looked like incidents, like an ill-managed rage of which he immediately repented falsely asking for forgiveness, and sometimes even kneeling. Then, once he understood just how submissive she'd got, those occasional fits of violent anger turned into beatings. The plead for forgiveness was replaced by further verbal harassment. He knew she would have no place to seek refuge from him. She was his thing, his property, an object, sometimes an ornament, with the advantage that, when she broke, she'd always heal, eventually. When she replayed in her head, his beatings and the trivial reasons they would follow, she shivered in horror, her body seizing, tormenting her with the memories of all that violence. And then, with time, she had become used to it. It had become inevitable as well as it was inevitable that she'd think back to those events and relive those painful memories. Sometimes she would provoke his wrath with small acts of rebellion, as a result of which he would take the broom and hit her until she'd collapse to the ground, screaming in pain. Then, and only then, he'd stop. Not because of some weird kind of remorse, but because he feared that the neighbours would hear the cries. Several times he'd take her by the neck and, a hand covering her mouth, he'd use her like a punching-ball, hitting around her kidneys to make it hurt even more. Then he'd take her by the hair and drag her to the basement, to stifle the noise of her screams and, still unsatisfied, he'd kick her in her stomach until she'd throw up. Then, he'd lock her there, exhausted and shivering in the dark, among damp rags and detergents, until the following morning, when he demanded that breakfast be served.

That was it. Exhausted and horrified by those terrible memories she was about to get up to start cooking dinner when she got a message on the phone he'd given her for that sole purpose. He wrote, in so many words, that he and the child wouldn't come home for dinner. She didn't know how to react. On one hand, she felt relief. Not having him home meant tranquillity. On the other hand, she knew that, when he wouldn't come home after work, he was with his lover, and she couldn't stand that he'd involve her son in it, as if they were a normal, happy family and she wasn't at home, waiting for them to return. His own happy family, the one in which she didn't exist. Now, the nightmare of the clock, of the passing time, of the duties, was over.

A breath of freedom, that would only last until they would be back: the son in an hour, him late at night, if he decided to come back before breakfast, at all. But nothing mattered any longer.

She was again instantly lost in her thoughts, and back in time.

One crucial moment of her life escaped her, and she couldn't manage all the confusion. From time to time, images appeared in her mind that remained latent, resembling more vivid dreams than real events that had once actually happened. In those images, she was in the Sacred Wood with the boy she had loved, that boy from the Village, his eyes fixed on her face, the tender caresses, the kisses, lulled by the music that could be heard only there. And then, nothing. In the following memory, she was in the Haunted Forest with him, the man whom she'd married. They were making love on the ground, but how they had come to this, she had no idea. It was the night when his seed had made her pregnant, giving its fruit, the only reason of her life, the only reason for her to stay there, in that house, with that man, the only person she felt she loved above all else, the only being which gave a logical sense to the unworthy life she led. Her son. But the situation, unfortunately, had deteriorated. Ever since he was a child, she'd always protected him with great care from his father's monstrosity, never doubting her role as his mother. But now, everything was changing. He was changing, and more often than not, she'd find herself unable to recognize him. As he grew older, his character evolved until he became more and more similar to his father's, first in his thoughts, then in his words, and she begun to fear that, sooner or later, he would start imitating his actions. It had taken her a long time to become aware of her son's changes. At first she couldn't see them at all, she loved him too much to believe that he was falling into his father's footsteps. And even when the first concrete signals came, she would just refuse to believe, justifying the boy as if everything was but an isolated behaviour that didn't really pertain to him. Only when the episodes became more and closer together, she had to concede that she'd been consciously blind to the matter, and that, as much as she'd tried to hide the truth from herself, a new monster was growing under her eyes, and she could no longer salvage him. Then came the despair, the silent tears in the night, the lies, and the excuses which she told herself to justify him. Finally, she dumped all the fault on her damned husband, who somehow was taking away the only thing she had in the world: her son. Not physically moving away from her, to another home, with him. Much worse. He had managed to infest the boy's heart with that impalpable, invisible and terrible molecule, bearing the name of hate. She would never have accepted for her son to be capable of hate. But she knew, she was aware, now, the closest witness of this terrible truth. A truth that she could not admit if not to blame him, the infamous man that had subjugated her. He was the cause to the fall of her beloved son, that poor, young innocent soul was but a victim. And even if his actions were often unacceptable, he was never guilty. It was all that monster's fault, that same monster who'd keep crushing her body, heart, and soul without reason.

She went back to think about the Village and the young man with whom she had lived the most beautiful time she could remember. If he hadn't so suddenly disappeared, leaving no trace, saying nothing to anyone, without saying goodbye… How different her life would have been. Where did he go? And, above all, why? He seemed so happy at the Village. What had he been hiding? To think of the pain his escape must have inflicted on his parents. Who knew, if he'd ever returned?

It had been many years since she'd heard anything of those people. Her husband had isolated her, pulled her away, and made everything in his power to mangle her memory of that group of madmen who lived as troglodytes in that faraway place, lost in the woods. He had brainwashed her: it made no sense, the way they lived, and he would never understand how her parents could have allowed her daughter to live in such poverty as they had. At first, she'd tried to reply that he was misrepresenting the facts, but he played smart and, after he had made her move away from her family and the Village, he worked on her brain day after day for years, slowly persuading her that it must have been her the one who remembered some edulcorated version of the truth. He managed to obtain even the help of her parents, who had left the community and detached from it to go back to a more suitable way of life and by then agreed with his opinion of them as meaningless, invading, disrespectful of culture and profiteers. A sort of sect

to stay away from. It was the only point on which he'd get along with her family. As for the rest, between him and his mother, there were continuous quarrels. She couldn't stand how he treated his wife, and for this reason, she'd stopped visiting the family, even renouncing to see his nephew, because of the behaviour of the boy's father. However, even though she only saw the surface of those behaviours, those would be enough to make her want to oppose her son, although with poor results. For some time now, the woman had lost all hope for the redemption of her son and often asked herself why poor Adele wouldn't leave him, already. She couldn't believe it to be about the boy. During her few encounters with him in the last months, she'd seen him become more and more like his father. The woman tormented herself, asking herself where she'd gone so wrong. She could not believe to have brought such a subject into the world. He was selfish, controlling, despotic and a slave driver. But she couldn't bring herself to help her daughter-in-law giving up her own son.
Adele had forgotten what it meant to be a woman, or perhaps she'd never truly known. Probably because she'd never had the opportunity to live it fully. That man had taken all from her, and she'd just let him do it. She hadn't realized that indulging him at the beginning, she would have worsened what she only suspected in her heart. Yes, maybe she had loved him, at some point. Maybe he'd been a crush, the interest of a moment. Or maybe that too was love, a different side of love that she didn't know. Of course, she knew she hadn't been able to control her

attraction towards him if even that had been true. Today she wondered, if it hadn't been him the reason they were together then if she had wanted it, had he ever been able to love her? She was convinced that man didn't know what the word love meant, let alone felt, neither now nor at the beginning.

Opportunist, troublemaker, rude, jerk, scurrilous, brutal, uncivilized. She had many adjectives to describe him, but she knew that others didn't see him that way. He was like the moon: he would always show the one face. At home a terrible ogre, outside a true gentleman, loving, helpful, kind, courteous, nice, funny. She hated him. Damn! He was odious. Shamelessly odious. And with the other women, a true macho, the butch for the batch: the classic male specimen who wants to be an alpha in any situation. Adorable father to all children, loving husband to all wives, caring lover to all women who had been so lonely, disappointed, abandoned, even for a moment. And then he'd come along. He'd be there, for anyone, always. And this was precisely one of the things that would confuse her, one of the many that had prevented her from being careful enough to protect herself and above all her son. The more he was available to friends, the less he was present at home, the more he was helpful to his superiors, the less he was present at home, the more he went out for his love affairs, the less he was present at home. The less he was present at home, the happier she was. But she didn't realize it was a false happiness. She was lying to herself, and what's worse, she was aware of it.

She constantly looked in her mind for moments, episodes, situations that had made her happy, for a chance to escape from the depression that oppressed her. She did not remember that her father had ever acted like the man she had married. Yes, he'd been gruff, stern, not very talkative. She remembered that he'd only rarely tell her that he loved her. But she knew that her father loved her. No matter how many times he said it out loud, the loving gestures of every day mattered, and above all the love and respect he had for her mother, who reciprocated in her own way. Of her mother, she remembered the infinite patience she had towards everyone, always. She was the pillar of their family. Her opinion always mattered, and she always had the last word. She was attentions and love condensed, which was all Adele needed when she was younger, although when she became a teenager she wished she hadn't known her, so embarrassed she was of her attentions in front of the friends and classmates. And now their relationship had deteriorated. Her mother stopped calling her every day, as she used to, for years. Now she'd call maybe once a month, for a few moments, to know if she was good and little more. He'd had something to do with this, too. At first, he'd bought his in-laws love with pleasantries. Once he understood the dynamics of her family, he'd started to slowly convince her father of the daughter's stupidity. Of course, he'd never say it out loud, but he kept commenting with him over some small, irrelevant family episodes, laughing about how silly and too much concentrated on futile things she was.

One, two, ten, a hundred, a thousand times he said the same idiocies until her father began to think that his son-in-law was right and that, maybe because he loved her and was her father, he'd just never noticed. Luckily, she'd married such a good and caring man that would hide, within the walls of his house, the faults of his daughter. So the father, just as his son-in-law had done with him, started to hint to his wife all the nonsense and silliness of their daughter. And after one, two, ten, a hundred thousand stories, the image of her daughter crushed in front of her eyes and even she began to doubt of the intellectual abilities of her child. In short, he had managed to convince them that they had given birth to a dumb girl, only to dump on him the burden of protecting her, even from herself. Obviously, this deteriorated the relationships between the parents and the daughter and isolated her even more. With the help of the distance, since they had lived in Donegal for some time before they moved, not fitting in with the ideologies of the people of the Village, to Dublin, while the daughter and her family were in London. Over time things had changed. Her mother had begun to feel that something was wrong, but she believed the daughter responsible for that feeling she couldn't understand. He was good at hiding his misdeeds and whenever his guilt would become apparent, he always had an excuse at the ready, sometimes exaggerated, but that became credible because it was confirmed by his wife, terrified of the consequences that she would have to endure if she ever told the truth. The father, however, would continue to believe him. Poor Adele was resigned and impotent facing the life she was living. It was not in her nature, but sometimes she would consider suicide as the only solution to end her miserable life. Then she would think better, and she would go on for her son. If she had failed him, who would have protected the one reason left for her to live? How could he grow up in that home, without her support? She hadn't realized yet back then, that she'd already lost him, that the boy no longer depended on her. She hadn't realized that her son was becoming the very opposite of what she'd wanted for him.

Sooner or later she would have to look in the mirror. At some point, she would have to realize that things were not going as she wanted. That moment was fast approaching. And then what? Poor Adele.

The wind caressing the foliage of the trees, the smell of freshly cut grass, the scent of wildflowers. Her memory of those months spent at the Village seemed to be from another world, another story, a completely different life. How she hoped she'd made a different choice. How many times had she wondered, what if she'd decided to stay, going against her father, challenging her husband, who wanted her out of there? What would have changed? When her parents had discovered her pregnancy, they hadn't thought twice about it. Fervidly religious, they immediately worried about the scandal and cursed the moment they had moved to that small Village. In their beloved Dublin, this wouldn't have happened. Their only daughter would never have had intercourse before marriage, if she'd been surrounded by civility in the Irish capital, never. It was an anachronistic mentality, a legacy of older times or the dullness of people who watched and judged their neighbours constantly, without realizing that everyday life can touch them, too. In any case, a was necessary. That young boy with a safe job, and didn't waste his time with frivolous studies, was the best solution. He would never deny his son. Abortion wasn't ever an option. Not even worth mentioning. In truth, it was a subject that she didn't want to face, either. Although for different reasons than those of her old-fashioned parents, she wouldn't have done it. And in a sense, the people of the Village had been one of the reasons dispelling that idea. Every newborn was more than welcome and, although accepting and respecting the choices of each of the future mothers, all in the villagers' lives led to one direction: the cultivation of an existential culture, a hymn to life. This didn't mean that everything was well, that no one quarrelled or that nobody ever cried, no. It was a place like any other, yet so different.

Every time she looked for a happy memory, whether it came from more remote or more recent moments in time, the birth of her child, the wedding day, the arrival to her new home, her thoughts always brought her back to that Village. To that group of friends, sworn to eternal brotherhood, to the races in the meadows, to the playful way they used to execute their work. It was another world. Another world completely. Many years had gone by, and even though her thoughts went back from time to time, she felt sure that nothing remained of that place. This certainty didn't come from her. It was her husband, first insulting those people in harsh and hateful tones, then reporting to her the false news, several times, in different instances, he'd hinted of having read somewhere that there was nothing left of that community, that in a few years even the most avid supporters of that crazy utopia had surrendered to reality, realizing that what they were pursuing wan an unattainable idea. She was the only one stupid enough to still believe in those fairy tales. Her husband hadn't stopped there. He had slowly made disappear all the objects around the house that linked Adele to the Village. He had taken them from under her nose without her noticing. His plan had almost succeeded, but he could never take away from her the very last shreds of the Village: her own memories. Those memories, though faded, were still alive in her mind. And even if the objects, the photographs, and the phone number of the Great High Priestess went missing, he could not erase them from her brain.

She wondered what she could eat. She already knew that, what she wouldn't cook that night, he would want to eat the following day. He usually left her the crumbs, the crust of the bread and the bones of the flesh to eat, after he and his son had eaten. So that evening she would fast. A tea brewed from the weeds she had torn from the garden and, if anything had ever escaped the despot, she'd try and take a piece of old bread from the bag for the kennel, another gesture that showed to the community his great generosity. To make sure that she wouldn't eat it, he weighed it every day, with a manic attitude.

Sometimes he'd accuse her of stealing the bread from that bag, even when it wasn't true, only because he couldn't remember how much it weighed the night before. And to make sure that she wouldn't touch it, he insulted and punished her in front of her son, depriving her of the food from his table and kicking her out of the kitchen as if she were unworthy of sitting with them. When such atrocities happened, she smiled at her son, as if nothing had happened, as if everything he'd just seen were normal.

It was precisely this attitude what had strengthened in the boy the idea that his father's way of treating her mother was the way to go with all women. He wasn't his life model, though. He was not stupid and he'd understood how to survive living with him at home, which meant not getting his ass kicked by that violent man. He enjoyed a special state of grace, though. He was his trophy, his legacy, and because of this he never twisted a hair on his head. She? She loved him infinitely, as a mother loves a son, and more because she also loved him as the only reason to survive the abuse of that monster. For this same reason, her love for his son appeared exaggerated, morbid, sick to the few who visited the house. And often they would criticize her in front of her husband, not knowing what that may cause. So the rare visits of her husband's friends always ended, once they would leave the house, in furious quarrels and beatings. He could not invite his friends to his own house because she shamed him with her behaviour, her simplicity, her speaking out of turn, her looking at someone, her lack of education and manners –

according to him. Fortunately, it had been months since he had invited anyone, the truth was, many of his friends had decided not to go there anymore. He thought it was because of his wife. He did not notice that they were all turning away from him because of his horrible character. Something had shone through the crevices of his mask. Some had seen part of what he really was, and not many could stand him, anyway. And they didn't even know half of what he was at home.

While she was considering what to eat, a second message arrived:

"Don't you dare touch tonight's dinner. Cook it tomorrow night. Your shitty tea is good enough for you, and stop ruining the lawn of my garden or I'll make you pay for it! Fast and die! We'll dine on a tasty paella… Green of envy, are you? That's right! "

She was used to that language, she was used to fasting, she was used to being oppressed like that. But what she didn't know was that his son had written that message. Certainly encouraged by the father, inspired by his jealous lover, but still, he'd sent it, while at the table, drinking the second beer his father bought him and perhaps not completely aware of what he was doing, victim of the treacherous games of a sick man who held his empire trough anger and terror. That evening, a cold wind was blowing and soon, it started to rain. She hurried to close the windows. Those five minutes of agitated distraction proved useful to her soul. She took her cracked teapot from the cupboard, set it on the stove, and infused a handful of weeds, those damn weeds she picked up in the garden after she'd mowed the lawn. Then she added a licorice stick she'd managed to stole from the jar in the pantry. Once the tea was ready, she sat down again at the table, turned on the television keeping the volume very low to be able to hear the noise of the bike or the car when they would have come home, and have time to turn it off and escape to her room, where she was supposed to keep whenever he was at home and she wasn't cooking for him. When he arrived, the first thing he did was to put his hand on the television to see if it was hot. She didn't have the right to use it. He made the money and he did what he wanted with it. Since nothing in that house was hers, she mustn't use anything, and he thought the money gave him the right to order her around, giving her next to nothing and saying it was what she was worth for.

The day was over. She took the last sip, then carefully washed the cup, wiped it, and put it back in the cupboard. Then, she turned off the lights and went to the bedroom. Exhausted, she wore the simple dressing gown that had been white a decade ago, worn to the point of looking like a rag. It was all she had to wear: her wardrobe was empty. He'd thrown away her clothes and never bought them back. Unfortunately, to all of this, she was accustomed, addicted, to the point of thinking, in the darkest times, that it was normal, that all the women of the earth, sooner or later, would suffer her destiny. She knew it was not the truth, though. The television had shown her that a woman did not have to accept to live that way, the television had suggested her so many possible solutions, and it had made it clear that her husband was an ignoble monster. She sighed deeply. The image of his son distracted her from those thoughts. She untied her hair, lay down on the cold bed, covered herself with a blanket and, after begging her gods for a better life, she went to sleep. Goodnight, Adele.

End of CELTIC, the Prequel vol.1

Printed in May 2018
by Youcanprint *Self-Publishing*